THE TERRIBLE PRESENCE—

I screamed and tried to run away, but my feet were weighted. I could not move, nor could I escape his hands as they fastened around my throat, pressing, while I cried out a second time, while I coughed and gagged and moaned, striving to be free. But between me and the moonlight was the shadow with the hands, the hands that were still clamped around my aching throat, shutting off air and sound and sight. And as everything around me dimmed, I had only one final frightened thought: *So this is how it ends. The curse has claimed me for its own at last.* . . .

SIGNET Gothics You'll Enjoy Reading

☐ **IDES OF NOVEMBER by Florence Stevenson.** What grim specter of fate pursued her, reaching out to steal her away from life and her chance for love . . . ? (#Q6370—95¢)

☐ **DARK ODYSSEY by Florence Stevenson.** Caught in the peril of the ancient ruins, her love was threatened by echoes from the forbidden past. . . . (#Q6223—95¢)

☐ **BIANCA by Florence Stevenson and Patricia Hagan Murray.** Could an old house destroy a beautiful marriage? What was the forgotten tragedy which brought sorrow to all who dwelt within the aged mansion? (#T5434—75¢)

☐ **THE CURSE OF THE CONCULLENS by Florence Stevenson.** A beautiful young woman ignores intimations of seduction and doom—to become the governess in an accursed Irish castle. (#T4903—75¢)

☐ **THE WINTER KEEPER by Jeanne Crecy.** Had the silent snows trapped her in their shrouded world of doom . . . ? (#Q6472—95¢)

☐ **MANSION OF PERIL by Caroline Farr.** Could love protect her from the terror that ruled the gloomy, ancient castle . . . ? (#Q6328—95¢)

THE NEW AMERICAN LIBRARY, INC.,
P.O. Box 999, Bergenfield, New Jersey 07621

Please send me the SIGNET BOOKS I have checked above. I am enclosing $_____(check or money order—no currency or C.O.D.'s). Please include the list price plus 25¢ a copy to cover handling and mailing costs. (Prices and numbers are subject to change without notice.)

Name_____

Address_____

City_____State_____Zip Code_____
Allow at least 3 weeks for delivery

A Shadow on the House

by Florence Stevenson

A SIGNET BOOK
NEW AMERICAN LIBRARY
TIMES MIRROR

COPYRIGHT © 1975 BY FLORENCE STEVENSON

All rights reserved

SIGNET TRADEMARK REG. U.S. PAT. OFF. AND FOREIGN COUNTRIES
REGISTERED TRADEMARK—MARCA REGISTRADA
HECHO EN CHICAGO, U.S.A.

SIGNET, SIGNET CLASSICS, MENTOR, PLUME AND MERIDIAN BOOKS
are published by The New American Library, Inc.,
1301 Avenue of the Americas, New York, New York 10019

FIRST PRINTING, JUNE, 1975

1 2 3 4 5 6 7 8 9

PRINTED IN THE UNITED STATES OF AMERICA

… **Part** …

ONE

My life has changed so amazingly in the last three years that I can scarcely believe that all that happened really did happen, and since I am still having trouble trying to understand myself and those actions which brought me so close to disaster, I have decided to write it all out. Now that the new nurse has come, I am easier in my mind and can fix my attention for more than just a few minutes at a time. I know that much of what I shall write will be painful for me to set down, but still, even at the cost of great mental anguish, I shall tell the entire truth about myself. It is only through self-knowledge that we grow, a doctor of mine has said. Yet, I do wish that . . . No matter, I shall begin. . . .

I must admit that the vicissitudes that have befallen me were of my own making—some of them, at least. I have always been headstrong and ambitious, but on the other hand, how could I not be ambitious when possessed of such a remarkable singing voice—a true *lirico-spinto* of astonishing range and quality. Perhaps if I had not been so gifted, I should have been content to settle down in Denver and live happily ever after with any one of the dozen boys who sought my favors and whom I ignored so studiously that my brother Esau called me "stuck up." I have never been stuck up. Since that moment when Paulina da Costa heard me sing and gave me her candid opinion of my capabilities, I have merely been aware of my own true worth. I am not conceited; I am merely realistic.

I suppose I should explain how I happened to meet

Paulina. Our encounter was, I believe, predestined, for a friend of mine has said that when a person has a God-given talent such as mine, God also provides a way for it to be discovered, tutored, and displayed. Thus, the first link of that chain of events leading to our meeting was forged before I was born.

It all started in Lynn, Massachusetts, when Mama, then nineteen and the daughter of a poor but worthy Presbyterian clergyman, met Alexander MacKenzie, another clergyman lately come from Aberdeen. It was his desire to travel westward and settle in one of the frontier towns, where he could, hopefully, build a church and a congregation at the same time. He was an enthusiastic young man, full of zeal and fire. He spoke well and he looked well—in fact, he was extremely handsome; it proved an irresistible combination, and within three months of their first meeting, he and Mama were married. Scarcely had they shaken the rice from their shoes than they were on a train bound for Cleveland, the first but not the last of their many stops.

Of course, I do not remember our early peregrinations, but I have some idea of them because Mama has talked about them enough, describing Papa's dissatisfaction with practically every town between Boston and Denver with a dry disdain which would probably have been very dampening to Papa had he been alive to hear her. He had, however, died in Denver a year after we arrived there. Papa had hoped to attach himself to one of the several Presbyterian churches in town, or, failing that, to move on to California—but the fate that has shaped my life intervened, and he died of some type of fever. Mama was left with a three-year-old child (me) and a babe-in-arms—my brother, Esau—no savings, and—her father and sole remaining parent having died two years back—no way of returning to Lynn. Fortunately, she was exceptionally attractive in those days, and she looked so lovely in her "weeds" that Mr. Bartlett, the undertaker, fell madly in love with her and not only paid for the entire funeral but married her six months later. She had, she often said in later years, never expected to marry a gentleman of that persuasion, but since she had her children to consider, she accepted.

I hardly remember Mr. Bartlett. Mama has said that he was of medium height with a fair complexion and blue eyes set in a plump face and that he had a brusque manner that concealed a very sensitive nature. He had never liked his calling, but it was lucrative because people were always dying in Denver—in fact some of them came there to die or to try to extend a disease-shortened span which invariably ended sooner rather than later. Involved in the business with Mr. Bartlett were his older brother, Edward, and his younger sister, Cynthia—a dark melancholy-appearing lady who, unlike her brother, absolutely adored funerals and played the harmonium at all the services. It was her habit of practicing her music on the piano in the house Mama and her husband shared with the rest of the family that led to the discovery of my own talent. One day, when I was not quite four, I astonished her and my mama by playing "Nearer my God to Thee" with commendable accuracy, even though I had never touched the piano before. Not only did I use my left hand to provide chords for the melody, but I sang the tune on-key and in a sweet true voice. It was a performance that led my Aunt-by-marriage Cynthia to clap her hands and inform Mama that I would be an asset at funerals before I was much older. Fortunately or unfortunately as the case may be, I was never recruited for these duties, since six months later, my stepfather, overseeing preparations for a burial, tripped on a spade and fell into the open grave, hitting his temple on a corner of the coffin. He died instantly.

Though at the time I was inconsolable over the loss of the piano, subsequent events proved the occasion to be fortuitous rather than tragic, for if Mama had not decided to use the money she had inherited from Mr. Bartlett's portion of the business to buy a large old house on the opposite side of town and turn it into a boarding establishment, she never would have met Mr. Da Costa and, through him, Paulina, his sister. I used to be positive that it was God's hand that thrust Mr. Bartlett over the brink, though when I mentioned this to Mama, she grew astonishingly angry and said I was most dreadfully selfish. Actually, now that I think about it, perhaps I was, but without my stepfather's unfortunate accident, I should never have met Paulina—or Lina as I soon learned to call her—and it was she who was responsible for launching me into the world of opera. Even before that, she had changed my entire life—yet when she arrived, which happened to be two days after my tenth birthday, it is a wonder she did not hate me on sight. I know I was prepared to hate her because Mama had recruited me to help her ready the second-floor front—Conchita, our maid, being inexplicably absent. If I shut my eyes, I can remember exactly how I looked and, alas, exactly how I acted.

At ten, I was thin, with long legs that seemed to get longer every day, or at least that was how Mama phrased it, for my skirts were always needing to be lengthened. I had a thin face, which seemed to be all eyes; these were a peculiar shade that I preferred to call green but which my brother, Esau, a great trial to me at all times, described as "mostly yeller, like a cat's." My hair, which I wore in two tight pigtails, was red, but despite Esau's contention, I was not a carrot-top—it wasn't orangy, but on the chesnut side. My features were good—I knew that for a fact because our boarders were always telling Mama that I would be a beauty when I grew up.

I might mention that I could hardly wait to grow up. People often talk about the "innocent joys" of childhood, but I can only think they must have short memories. I was never joyful as a child; I was bored by school, by other children, and by the monotony of my daily existence, which contained more than its quotient of adults patting me on the head and saying to Mama, "Isn't she a dear little girl! My goodness, Mrs.

Bartlett, you do have such charming children—both of them are so adorable."

These empty compliments were often tendered to Mama in lieu of money owed for lodgings, the idea being to keep her talking in the hall while trunks were lowered from windows or family members sneaked down the back stairs, but though she was often quite aware of these devices, my brother and I were never allowed to make faces or indulge in other antagonistic behavior—it was necessary, Mama insisted, for us to set an example. For whom and why were topics on which she never elucidated, but deviations from what she considered proper conduct brought retaliation in the form of missed suppers and painful sessions in the barn. Consequently, being good was a habit with us— at least in her presence—but on the day Paulina da Costa arrived, I could not really contain myself, for I was terribly disappointed. I had been a member of our Sunday School choir for several months, and it was the main joy of my existence, especially since I was often given little solos to perform. One of these was to be sung the following Sunday, but due to Conchita's absence, Mama had compelled me to miss practice, which meant that Jane Stuart would be given my solo even though she invariably sang flat. I knew I was inviting trouble, but I did not scruple to let Mama know exactly how I felt. When we made the bed, I jerked the sheets about. When I brought the fresh flowers into the room, I slammed the vase down on the table and I did not even care when the water spilled and I had to wipe it up. I was glad because it had made a spot on the carpet of the horrid room where the horrid lady was going to stay!

I was so cross that I had quite forgotten I had liked her brother, Mr. Angelo da Costa, very much Billed as the Amazing Angelo, he was a magician and a hypnotist and he could do the most delightful tricks. Though Mama had been warned by her ex-in-laws never to take in theatrical people, she had always ignored these strictures. I am of the opinion that as a clergyman's daughter and relict, she was secretly attracted by the forbidden, having had so much of the "bidden" in her lifetime; and certainly the performers who stayed with us were more interesting than the salesmen, schoolteachers, and other lodgers who came to us—and who, I might add, began to avoid us after Mama opened her doors to members of the theatrical profession. Indeed, I can remember being lectured at school by well-meaning teachers on the folly of mixing with these debased men and women, and there were even certain parents who forbade their children to associate with Esau and myself. I like to believe that their progeny were the losers!

Angelo da Costa had remained with us three weeks before moving on to Colorado Springs, and we were sorry to see him go. It was several months later that Mama heard from Paulina, his sister, who had written that she needed to come to Denver for reasons of health and that she might be staying indefinitely. Mama had not been overly enthusiastic about receiving an invalid into her house, but she had been fond of Mr. Da-Costa, and as I have said, fate must have played its part in her decision. I do wish I had been more aware of fate at that time—I still blush when I recall my greeting to my mentor-to-be. She arrived before Mama had finished the room, and it was my duty to admit her—something I did with the ill-grace that had characterized all my actions that morning. In answer to the pealing of our front-door bell, I stomped down the stairs and pulled the door open, letting it bang against the wall with a force that rattled the windows on either side of it.

"My goodness!" A small woman in a dark suit looked at me with startled eyes.

I glared up at her—actually, I was nearly on eye-level with her, since I was tall for my age and she was so small. "Come in," I growled, "Mama's nearly done with your room."

"Thank you." Smiling at me pleasantly, she stepped over the threshold, but as I started to slam the door, she caught it from me and shut it softly, "No more loud noises, please. My ears have been battered enough by my long train journey." I felt a flush mount to my cheeks, but before I could mutter an apology, she continued, "You have the temperament as well as the voice, I see."

"V-voice?" I stuttered, wondering if I could have heard her correctly.

"My brother Angelo tells me you have a voice," she continued. "You are Leila MacKenzie, are you not? Do you mind if I sit down? I am a bit exhausted." Without waiting for my answer, she sank into a chair in the hollow of the stairs and looked at me steadily. "Yes, you are this child my brother mentioned. He described you well—the hair, the eyes, the passion. Well, it is good—an artist must have the passion, but she must channel it and not let it master her." She smiled at me, and I, staring into her black, luminous eyes, wondered if she were teasing me, as adults often did; but her words had not been teasing or patronizing. As I regarded her doubtfully, she continued, "I do want to hear you sing."

"You . . . you do?" I faltered.

"It is one of the reasons I came," she said. "Because my brother told me about you."

She had to be teasing me! Half-angrily, I cried, "But your brother never heard me sing!"

"Oh, yes," she said positively, "to your kitten on the porch one afternoon. Do you know that many years ago in Sweden a little girl sang to her kitten, and someone heard her. She was taken to the Royal Opera House in Stockholm to study, and when she grew up, she became a great artist. Her name was Jenny Lind."

"Jenny Lind," I breathed. "Ohhhhh."

"You've heard of her?" she demanded.

"She was married to her husband in Boston," I said glibly, and Mama has told me that my grandfather had her to sing in his church. Mama was not born at the time but her mama said that Miss Lind had the voice of an angel!"

Miss Da Costa nodded. "It is what I have heard, too. And so your grandfather had the great Jenny Lind to sing in his church—and now his granddaughter . . . oh, I must hear you. I am excited as I have not been in many months!" Her black eyes were somber. "Now that I myself am forbidden to perform, I need an interest. I hope my brother was right about you—he has a good ear for an amateur. I shall look forward to listening to you. Indeed, I can hardly wait."

"You need not wait!" I cried. "Listen to me! Listen now!" Without further ado, I began to sing the hymn I would have performed at choir that afternoon. As I concluded it, Mama came running down the stairs.

"Leila MacKenzie!" she gasped. "Have you gone stark raving crazy?"

"Indeed she has not!" Paulina da Costa jumped from her chair and threw her arms around me. "My brother was right! It is there! And it is good. I shall begin to live again!"

Mama opened her mouth, then closed it again. I saw a look of concern in her eyes. Doubtlessly, she thought Paulina da Costa crazy, too. However, she said gently enough, "Miss Da Costa, you are looking far from well. Might I get you a glass of water?"

Paulina drew back from me, and for the first time, I saw that she was very pale and that she had pressed a hand to her chest, as if it pained her; but she shook her head. "No, it is only the rigors of the journey. I have come such a long way, and then to find such happiness, such excitement! It is more than I expected —more even than my brother led me to believe. I have found gold, Mrs. Bartlett, a vein of pure gold." She put her thin hand on my mother's arm. Beseechingly, she whispered, "Will you let me have this child—to teach?"

I think I ceased to breathe as I waited for Mama's answer, but I think that Mama was actually afraid to refuse, for indeed Paulina did look ill, even feverish. There was a hectic flush on her high cheekbones and dark hollows under her eyes. Mama said pacifically, "Why, yes. If you think my daughter has talent, I should like it to be nurtured—young women ought to have accomplishments."

"Accomplishments!" Paulina actually snorted. "To play prettily upon the piano, to paint china, to warble little ditties—these are accomplishments. But to sing as your daughter will sing is to reach the heights, the verp pinnacle of the artistic profession."

"Profession?" Mama repeated. "You mean that Leila would sing for money?"

"For money—for the world's riches!" Paulina exclaimed.

Mama looked dubious and even stern. "I have never thought of my daughter going into the theater. . . ."

"I have!" I cried. "Oh, Mama, I have. I should love it above all things to be another Jenny Lind!"

"Another Jenny Lind!" Much to my anger, Mama laughed heartily. "Listen to us! Aren't we talking nonsense—to speak of my daughter in such a context when she is only a little girl!"

Paulina da Costa leaned forward, and her eyes seemed to burn into my mother's face as she said, "This is a little girl, yes—but she has a great future in her throat, Mrs. Bartlett!"

Looking back on that scene now, ten years later, I can hardly believe the meeting happened as I have told it; but it did, and as I have said, it transformed my life. One moment I had been a sulky child—the next I had become an artist with a temperament and a teacher. Fate again.

Oddly enough, I have never really liked to ascribe the advent of Paulina da Costa to the workings of fate, for if that were true, I should be in some way responsible for the asthma that wrecked her own career. Indeed, much as I profited by our association, I have always been sincerely sorry that the music world was robbed of Paulina's talents. She was a true artist, with a wonderfully expressive face, superb acting ability, and such a feeling for music! How marvelously she sang even simple little ballads like "Annie Laurie" and "Flow

Gently, Sweet Afton"! Even Mama recognized her excellence, though it was a long time before she would agree with Paulina that I too would make my mark in music. I resented her attitude when I was younger, but I understand her now. Unlike Paulina, she had not learned to trust her own ear—she thought I had a pretty voice, but even after Paulina's enthusiastic reaction, she did not quite comprehend its true worth. I do not hold it against her anymore; had a Mozart been born to a dirt farmer instead of into a musical family, he too would have had a hard road to hoe—I mean no pun. Yet I am sure that had Mozart been born in such obscurity, he too would have found a Paulina to raise him from the dust—true artistry cannot long be hidden.

Despite the advent of Paulina, my artistry remained hidden longer than I liked. After being momentarily wafted to the heights, there was a diminishing of excitement and the beginning of a routine, which I would call variously taxing, tedious, impossible! For years, I sang nothing but scales—hours of up and down the piano, hours of learning to breathe, to focus the tone, to sight-sing. There were nights when I dreamed of notes starting from the pages and buzzing about my head like an angry swarm of bees. There were times when I longed to throw my exercise books at Lina's feet and scream at her in the idiomatic Italian she was teaching me, but though she had praised my temperament, I dared not display it in her presence. I had done it once, and she had merely locked up the piano she had had shipped from New York, put the music away, and ordered me from her room. She did not speak to me for a week, and oddly enough nor did Mama; even Esau avoided me, for though he was not in the least musical, he adored Paulina. Everybody did—our guests, the people from the neighborhood, even the disapproving Bartletts. During that week, I lived in limbo—no, deprived of my lessons, I did not live, I merely existed, and finally, after much weeping and many apologies, she deigned to forgive me and the scales started again. But there was a difference—I now treated her with even more respect, having realized how very bleak life was without her.

There was a difference in her attitude, too. Perhaps she had realized that though discipline is the most important lesson a singer must learn, a child growing up in a town where the emphasis is less on culture than on mining needs to know where her work will take her. Accordingly, she began to tell me wonderful stories of her experiences in opera, and about her artist friends in New York, from whom she was always receiving long, chatty, affectionate letters full of back- and front-stage gossip.

It was tremendously exciting for me to hear about the performance when Jean de Reszke, returning to the Metropolitan for a *Lohengrin,* received a half hour of sustained applause before he could continue with his aria. Of course, I was more interested in the sopranos Melba and Sembrich—and I was surprised to learn how bitterly the critics had reacted to the new opera, *Tosca,* describing its heroine as depraved. They were equally bitter about a work called *Messaline* with Emma Calvé, but Carlo Benedetto—whose father, Maestro Nicolo Benedetto, managed one of the more prestigious traveling opera companies—wrote that *Messaline* was nothing as an opera and it was only Calvé's acting and voice that saved it. Much to my surprise, he was unimpressed by the great Melba, saying that her acting was inept. However, in 1903 when the Italian tenor Caruso made his debut in *Rigoletto,* Mr. Benedetto had nothing but praise for his voice; much to my disappointment, he had hardly anything good to say about the female singers that season. I thought him far too critical—I much preferred to hear Paulina talk about the Metropolitan Opera House itself, with its red plush and gold interior, its immense chandelier, its tiers of seats reaching to the roof, its marvelous promenades and cafés, its glittering audiences. I heard about the tons of flowers flung at the feet of the reigning prima donnas, of the wealthy people who feted them and presented them with fabulous jewels—diamond tiaras, stomachers, rings, ropes of pearls, emerald or ruby brooches. I also heard how many of the artists married into the ranks of the millionaires or even the European nobility— Minnie Hauk had married a baron! My ambition took a new turn; I wanted to be a great prima donna, but I also wanted to marry either a millionaire or a "crowned head" and live in one of the palaces Paulina had described. I dreamed of a historic chateau in Normandy, a castle on the Rhine or the Thames, but I would have been equally pleased to own a mansion on Fifth Avenue or a Newport "cottage"; certainly, I was of the opinion that my small room in Mama's house was no place for a prima donna!

I kept these latter ambitions to myself, knowing instinctively that Paulina would never approve; the trappings she had mentioned meant nothing to her—though she might have had her share of them. It seemed odd to me that she had never married; before illness had marked her features and wasted her frame, she must have been lovely, and certainly she was charming, but once when I asked her about the lack of love in her life, she had laughed. "My love is my music—it has been my husband and my child. It is thus for many singers."

Singing might have been enough for Paulina, but there came a time when my incessant vocalizing did not suffice for me. How could I ever be a prima donna and marry a "crowned head" if I sang nothing but exercises and scales? I was nearly mad with frustration, and if I dared not parade my feelings before my teacher, no one else remained in ignorance as to my state of mind. I quarreled with my few friends and with Mama; Esau and I had several actual fist fights, and though I was fifteen and big for my age, Mama whipped me for being impertinent to a lodger. Nobody understood me; I hated everybody except Paulina, and I was even cross with her until the afternoon when I came into her room to find her seated at the piano, playing some of the loveliest music I had ever heard. For the moment, all my ill spirits fled.

"What is it?" I breathed.

"It is a score my brother sent me—a score of *La Bohème*."

"The opera Melba sings!" I exclaimed.

"Yes," she said. "Mimi."

"Who is Mimi?" I asked.

"I am," Paulina said softly, and in the merest thread of a voice she sang, "Mi chiamano Mimi"—"My name is Mimi." When she had finished, I was in tears.

"Oh, Lina." I clasped her hand. "It is so beautiful! Why do I want to cry?"

"Because you love it." She smiled at me mistily. "You will love it even more when you have learned it all."

"When will that ever be?" I sighed.

"We will start today. It might be a little difficult for you, but it lies within your range. It will be your first role."

I dropped her hand. Leaping to my feet, I jumped up and down clapping my hands and shrieking, "A role, a role, a real role?"

"Shhh." She put a finger to her lips. "Don't strain your cords. Yes, a real role and another and another—it's time."

My frustration vanished. I was happy again—completely happy—as under Lina's inspired coaching I learned in rapid succession Mimi, Violetta of *La Traviata*, Nedda of *I Pagliacci*, Zerlina of *Don Giovanni*, and Susanna of *Marriage of Figaro*.

Actually, the succession was not quite that rapid. During the time I was learning, I was also attending high school, where I gained some celebrity singing in school concerts. I was also promoted to chief soloist in our church. However, I remember very little about any activities outside of Paulina's room. I did creditably in school, but if you were to ask me who my teachers were, I could produce only a composite. As for my friends, I had very few among the girls, more among the boys, but none are memorable—how could they be to a prima donna with her eyes on mansions and moguls?

The only real memory I have of high school is of graduation night.

I was delighted to be leaving school. I was positive that this, my seventeenth summer, would mark a great turning point in my life. I would not only stop being a schoolgirl, I would become a professional singer—an artist! Where and how I was not sure, but it would come because I was ready. More than ready—I was bursting with impatience! I longed for the world Paulina had described so vividly. My voice was beautiful, and the mirror told me that I, too, was beautiful. There was one in the hall where we had our graduation dance, and on looking into it, I had almost not recognized the tall, slim girl with the masses of red-gold hair piled into an intricate pompadour, her tilted amber eyes aglow with excitement, her cheeks faintly flushed, and her full mouth slightly parted. I had run to the glass to stare at her. She had stared back at me in shock. "Is this me?" I had whispered incredulously.

"Watch out or you'll fall in, Miss Prima Donna!" A tall chunky boy in a tight coat had come to stand behind me. "It's my dance, I think, if you can tear yourself away."

Without a word, I moved into his arms, smiling up at him; inwardly, I was seething—hating him, hating all the silly boys in that room who had teased and mocked me for my ambitions. I was too good for them—there would come a time when they would boast that they had known me. I could hardly wait for the evening to end, but when it did and we all sang "Auld Lang Syne," I actually cried a little—but my tears had dried before I was out the door.

If I was ready for the Artistic Life on that June night of 1905, when I graduated, no one except me seemed aware of it. The very next day, I had an altercation with Paulina; I said I did not want to sing Susanna because she was a maidservant.

"If Melba can play such a maidservant, you should not complain," Lina told me tartly.

"But what are the costumes like?" I asked plaintively.

"Costumes!" she exploded. "What do they matter? Are you going to think about how you look or how you sound?"

I had visions of myself sweeping around the stage in velvets and laces sparked with jewels, but I said in a small voice, "Of course, I care most about my sound."

She gave me a long look. "I wonder if you do. I wonder if you really know what it is to be a singer. Sometimes I think I have painted far too rosy a picture. To sing in the studio is one thing—to perform on the stage is something else."

"I have performed for the whole school!" I reminded her.

"Yes, by yourself, but you would not be by yourself in an opera—there would be others and they would make difficulties for you, difficulties you cannot imagine. Artists can be terrible people, cruel, conniving, jealous. They would seek to undermine you and you would still have to sing, as if nothing were happening..."

"Yes, you've told me," I said a trifle impatiently, "but I know I shall be able to handle myself, and I have a voice." I looked at her pleadingly. "At least, you used to think so."

"Ah!" she clapped her hands. "Now you have pleased me, Leila."

"P-pleased you?" I faltered.

Putting her hand beneath my chin, she looked deep into my eyes, "Of late—since you have become a tall and lovely young lady—I have thought you entirely too satisfied with yourself, which is something an artist must never be. But today you have shown yourself to be not quite that confident—that is very good."

"Why is it good?"

"Because then you try harder, and to progress in any art, you must always try harder. You must never stop trying, my Leila, even though you do have your beautiful voice."

"Oh, Paulina—Lina." I clasped her hand. "Do you really think so?"

"I really do, child," she said softly.

"Then . . . why . . ." I began.

She raised her hand. "Not yet, my dear. However much you may think you are ready—you are not yet ready."

"When . . ." I began, and was silenced again.

"I will tell you," she said firmly. "Now—let us return to Susanna, who does wear a most beautiful wedding dress in the last act."

She did not refer to our conversation again, nor did I receive any more compliments from her that entire summer. In fact, the span of time from June to September was like any other summer—I helped Mama about the house, I went on picnics or horseback riding or swimming at the lake, and there were my daily lessons. I think I suffered more during those two and a half months than I ever had before. With a sort of ritualistic despair, I crossed off each day on my calendar, and each time I did it, I murmured "When?" until it was September 2—the second most important day in my life.

It did not begin that way. In fact, it bade fair to be the most awful day of my life—cataclysmic, indeed! The worst came first. I remember I was on my way out the door bound for I forget where when Mama suddenly bounced out of the parlor, dusting cloth in hand, to say sharply, "Leila, I want to talk to you."

"Yes, Mama." I sighed, preparing myself for a scolding. "What have I done now?"

"Victor Davis!" she said inexplicably and proceeded to enlarge on the subject of a boy I had been dating mainly because he was so persistent. A lot of other girls envied his attentions to me. He was known as a "good catch," for he was the son of a prosperous liverystable owner who had recently converted to horseless carriages—which Victor insisted was the "coming thing," though I had angered him on occasion by remarking that it was a pity they were not the "going thing" since we were always stalling. I had been seeing him all summer, but I had never let him hold my hand, so he certainly had no right to dare ask Mama if he could pay his addresses to me!

"He has to be crazy, Mama," I said when I had finished laughing.

"It's not funny, Leila." She frowned. "If you thought that, you shouldn't have encouraged him."

"I didn't encourage him!" I said hotly. "He knows that I want nothing except to sing."

"What about all the drives you've taken with him?"

"That's because it was fun going in the cars, not because of *him*. I shouldn't have minded if—if it'd been a—a horse or—or a white rabbit who was driving. So there!"

"You are so selfish, Leila." She sighed. "You don't think about anybody except yourself. One of these days, you're going to have a very rude awakening. One of these days . . ."

"Oh, Mama," I begged, "please don't lecture me. I am really surprised at Victor's thinking I'd be interested in him when all I've ever talked about is singing. He knows how important it is to me. He knows . . ."

"Your singing is important only to you, Leila—it is not the concern of the entire world!" Mama retorted.

"It will be!" I cried. "One day, it will be."

She sighed. "Oh, Leila, I don't think I've helped you any by encouraging you in this folly. So many young women hope to succeed—so many are doomed to disappointment. If you did marry a nice boy like Victor . . ."

"A nice boy like Victor!" I repeated in horror-stricken accents. "I would rather fall down dead in front of you, Mama! How could you even think I would be interested in the likes of Victor Davis? I shall marry a—a Vanderbilt or—or a Lord, if I deign to marry anyone!"

There was a loud burst of satirical laughter behind me. "Listen to her Royal Highness—will you just listen!" Esau jeered.

"You shut up!" I shrilled.

"Make me?" he invited, sticking his tongue out at me

and commencing to perform a war-dance around me, chanting, "Wait until I tell Victor—he'll never take you riding with him again."

"You tell him and I'll break your neck!" Flinging myself at him, I pushed him over backward. As he fell, I leaped on top of him, beating at him with my fists. "I hate you, I hate you, I hate you!" I yelled, meaning every word of it, hating him, hating home, hating everything in my frustration.

"Leila . . . Esau . . ." Mama cried. "Stop it! Stop it this instant!"

My brother, who was small and wiry, wriggled away from me and, flailing out furiously, hit me in the eye. Then he dashed out of the room while I shrieked in agony as bright starry flashes seemed to go off in my head.

"He's b-blinded me!" I wailed.

"Nonsense, he has given you only a black eye—or as they call it, a shiner, yes?" someone said in richly accented English.

The voice came from somewhere above my head. Dazedly, I looked up and with my good eye saw a young man standing in the middle of the hall, smiling at me. He was more elegantly dressed than anyone I had ever seen in Denver. His clothes were well-fitting and of a material I did not recognize. He wore a straw hat, tilted at a jaunty angle, and he carried a cane, his skin was a clear olive, his eyes large and brown, and when he removed his hat, which he did in another instant, he proved to have dark wavy hair. He looked at Mama apologetically. "You will excuse me that I have walked in, but I rang the bell and no one answered and since your door was open . . ."

Mama flushed. "As you see, I was occupied."

He smiled. "Often, when I was at home, I was similarly occupied as peacemaker between my young brother and sister. Children are the same the world over, no?"

I had scrambled to my feet. My eye hurt, my head throbbed, and from the way my cheeks burned, I knew

A Shadow on the House

I was blushing furiously. I am not a child!" I cried angrily, glaring at him and finding that I was practically as tall as he—which, though it might have helped to prove my point, added to my confusion.

"Leila," Mama said coldly, "go to your room."

"Leila?" the man echoed. "You are the Signorina Leila?" He looked at me doubtfully, even incredulously.

"Carlo!" Paulina exclaimed from the head of the stairs. "It is not possible!"

"Lina, *carissima!*" Running lightly up the stairs, he embraced her exuberantly.

They broke apart at once and Paulina, clinging to his arm, said, "But you must meet Mrs. Bartlett and —Leila, your eye, it is all red!"

"And will soon be all black," the man she had called Carlo said. "Do you have beefsteak in your icebox, Mrs. Bartlett?" he asked.

Mama nodded. "Yes, I do." She looked at me. "Go into the kitchen and apply it to your eye, Leila," she ordered. She shook her head. "I hardly know what to say about such conduct. I do not know what you must thing, Mr. . . ."

"Benedetto," Lina supplied. "Carlo Benedetto of the Benedetto Opera Troupe."

As I heard the introduction, I nearly fainted. Certainly the hall reeled around me dizzily and I saw at least two Mr. Benedettos. I remembered his name all too well—he was the critical Carlo Benedetto, who with his father managed that very prestigious traveling company!

"Leila"—Mama broke into my frenzied thoughts— "go and attend to your eye—it's swelling."

"Yes," I mumbled. I fled from the room, but when I reached the kitchen, I did not go near the icebox. Instead I flung myself, weeping, down on the floor, knowing I had made a spectacle of myself and knowing, too, that one of my cherished hopes had been forever blasted. I would never follow in Paulina's footsteps—I would never sing for the Benedetto Opera Troupe, anywhere, anywhere, anywhere! The way he had looked at me and said my name suggested that Paulina had written to him about me and that that was why he might have come—to hear me. And what had he seen and what would he think? My life was ruined. I wanted to die!

"Ah, I thought so—but you must put the steak on your eye, Leila." Paulina had come into the kitchen and now she hurried to the icebox and, opening it hastily, rifled through it. "Ah, here it is." She came to me with a slice of raw meat in her hand. "Carlo is right, it will swell—but this will make it more comfortable." She gently pressed the meat against my throbbing eye. "It is not at an end, you know, and Carlo will hear you this afternoon. That is why he has come."

"Oh, no!" I wailed.

"Shhhhh, no more tears," she said softly. "He is on business in this part of the country—he is arranging a Western tour—so you must stop your weeping, child, or you will be in no condition to sing."

"But what must he think of me?" I groaned.

"He thinks you are a little girl," Paulina said, "and it is up to you to prove that you are a grown-up artist. If you can do it, it will be to your credit. If you cannot, you have no business to go on singing and I am finished with you."

I stared at her incredulously. She had a stern look in her eye and she had spoken with unaccustomed crispness. She continued, "You have heard the expression 'The show must go on'? Often, I have said to you that no matter what happens off-stage, no matter what disaster occurs—when there is a performance to sing, you sing. You sing if you are unhappy—if your parent has died or your child, as was the case with poor Marcella Sembrich, some years back, and you sing, too, if you have a black eye, your feelings are wounded, and you are dreadfully embarrassed. Carlo will not come a second time, Leila, so what do you say to me?"

Her words had coursed through my veins like fire. Jumping up, I said, "I will sing!"

Yet that same afternoon I stared into my mirror and wept softly. I had rested for two hours, I had bathed and changed my dress, and with Mama's grudging consent, I had dabbed her rice-powder over my bruised eye; but the darkness remained and there was a corresponding darkness in my soul. I had not seen Carlo Benedetto since our fated encounter that morning, and my heart failed me at the prospect of facing him again—yet I had to. I would have to sing for him in a matter of ... I glanced at the little enamel lapel watch Mama had given me for a graduation present. I would have to sing for him in ten more minutes. I couldn't! My voice would fail me, and if not my voice, my heart. I had made such a spectacle of myself! What must he think? My cheeks burned, my heart seemed to beat faster, and that quickened pulse was duplicated in my throat. Yet if I didn't sing for him ... I glanced out of my window and my eye fell on the distant Rockies, high, snow-powdered, stark against the vivid sky. Beautiful! commented all the people passing through Denver on their way to somewhere else. But to me, who had never gone beyond them, they were walls, the walls of a prison for which I had only one key—my voice; otherwise, I might very well stay in Denver for the rest of my life. I couldn't. I wouldn't! Striding out of my room, I ran lightly down the stairs and tapped on Lina's door.

"Come in," she invited in a laughter-filled voice.

Drawing a deep breath, I opened the door and hesitated at the threshold. Lina was at her piano and he stood behind her. He smiled at me. "Come in, please," he said.

I had grown cold and tense again. Moving stiffly inside, I crossed the room to stand in the hollow of the piano. "I'm ready," I said in a small tight voice.

"Ready for your execution, Maria?" he demanded, winking at Lina. "But you know she does look like Maria Stuarda—that glorious red hair, and so tall. I am told that the real Maria Stuarda was a giantess." He smiled at me. "I am glad you are not so high, for then

I should have to look up to you and that would be demoralizing for me."

"Carlo," Lina said laughing, "you do talk a great deal of nonsense."

"Always," he agreed. "Play the opening bars of something and let her sing for me."

Lina's hands moved on the keys and into my ears came the introduction of Violetta's aria "Ah fors' è lui," and just as I thought I could never find my voice, the introduction was at an end and it was my time to sing. Without thinking, I sang. When I finished the aria, I felt frozen again, afraid to look at either of them. I did not know how I had sounded—the notes, everything had sped away from me. I was standing in a sort of limbo.

Finally, he said, "How does your eye feel now?"

My heart plummeted. I had sung badly. He was not interested in me. He was making polite conversation. "It's all right," I said.

"Then, if it does not bother you too much, let me hear another aria. Do you know the end of *Traviata?*"

"She knows all of *Traviata.*" Lina said.

"Good." He nodded. "Sing the 'Addio' and this time you will look at me, please."

I thought . . . I do not know what I thought, but I obeyed him, looking at him as I sang the "Addio." He moved a slender hand in time to my music and soon I was following his beat. As I finished, he smiled broadly and, turning to Lina, said, "I knew I could trust you. You were quite right—vocally, she is ready."

I looked at him incredulously. I could not believe what I was hearing. "You . . . like my singing?" I whispered.

"Seven-teen years old." He shook his head. "Seventeen years old! Is that all? I can scarcely believe it."

"Yes." Lina smiled. "Such a voice as must not occur often in a generation."

"No, not often—but you had such a voice, my Lina."

"You are too kind," she demurred.

"You had the voice and the technique to go with it—

the Maestro has said so and I agree with him. Besides, I remember."

"You remember, Carlo?" She laughed. "You were so young when I stopped singing."

"Not so young that I had no ears. It was not so long ago, Lina—ten years."

"Twelve," she corrected. "And you were only . . ."

"Seventeen," he said. "The age of this little one, and she would know a voice if she heard it."

Her eyes widened. "Are you twenty-nine, Carlo? I can't believe it."

He shrugged. "Believe it." He laughed ruefully. "Believe, too, that I shall be thirty next March 25th."

"March twenty-fifth!" She laughed and counted on her fingers. "Seven more months. Enjoy the fact that you are still twenty-nine, my dearest Carlo—and looking much younger."

The smile left his eyes. "But sometimes I feel as if a century had passed over my head. Ah, this traveling, this traveling—we are the Flying Dutchmen of the roads, Lina—around and around we go."

"Ah, Carlo, it is the old story. You would like to conduct in other houses, yes?"

"Yes, and there have been opportunities."

"You've not told the Maestro?"

"Never."

"You are a good son, my dear."

"He has been a good father."

"Ah, yes, I know," she said softly. "The dear Maestro, I wish he had come with you—how I should like to see him again."

I had been listening with increasing impatience. As they conversed, they strayed further and further from the subject of myself. I could bear it no longer. I said, "Please, if I am ready, may I sing with your company?"

They laughed. "You see, she is all eagerness," Lina told him.

He looked at me gravely. "But does she know what it is to tour? A night here, a night there, cold theaters, bad hotels, bad food, and—for her—bad company. She is too young . . ."

"I am not too young!" I cried. "I'll be eighteen on December third! That's only two months . . . well, the day after tomorrow, it will be only two months and—and thirty days!"

They laughed together a second time. "Two months and—and thirty days!" Carlo echoed. "She is in even more of a rush than I."

Lina nodded. "She is impatient, yes. Well, one cannot blame her. I, too, was impatient once. But the question is of a chaperon. If her mother would travel with her, but . . ."

My heart sank. "Mama—but she wouldn't, Lina. She abhors traveling—she never would. Why do I need a chaperon?"

"Because you can't go alone," she said decisively. "It would not be proper. You know that yourself, Leila. A young, unmarried girl!"

"No, it would be impossible," Carlo agreed.

"Aren't there other women in the company?" I asked.

"None to care for a child of seventeen," Carlo said.

"Nearly eighteen!" I exclaimed. "I'm not a child!"

"A child who fights with her brother and gets a black eye." He laughed.

I glared at him, hating him. "You don't know why!" I cried hotly.

"Anger must have been the reason." He smiled at me with a superiority I resented bitterly. "But there are ways of showing displeasure that need not result in bodily injury. In our company are many people with explosive tempers. If all of them reacted as violently as you, our curtain would never rise."

"Am—am I to be—punished because—because—" My lip trembled, and against my will, tears came into my eyes.

"No, darling." Lina came to me and put her arms around me. "Carlo is only teasing you." She turned to him. "Let us resume the important part of this discussion—the chaperon. I will speak to her mother.

Perhaps she would consent to come for a few months—she might even like it."

"She wouldn't!" I exclaimed. "She hates traveling, I tell you. She had too much of it when my papa was alive."

"If there were a female relative," Carlo Benedetto said.

"I have no female relatives—none close to me except Aunt Cynthia, and she wants me to sing at funerals. There's no one close to me except—Lina." My heart gave a great leap. "Lina," I said excitedly, "why couldn't you be my chaperon? Mama would certainly trust you!"

"I?" She looked doubtful.

Carlo Benedetto's dark eyes gleamed. "Could you?" he demanded. "Oh, Lina, we would love to have you with us. Especially me—especially the Maestro."

"I should love to come," she said slowly, "but as you know, I'm not very well...."

"You came here because of the air, I know," he said. "The air is no different in Salt Lake, which is when we would need her. We'll spend two weeks in Salt Lake starting Monday, February twenty-sixth. We'll then travel to Sacramento for two more weeks, two weeks in Stockton and two in San Francisco—then *basta!* We'll be through mid-April. That is not a very long time, my Lina."

"Many people go to California for their health," I said. "We've had lodgers who've told me it's much more healthful there."

Carlo Benedetto nodded. "It is true—California is much like Italy, Lina."

"Italy . . ." she breathed. "How I should like to see Italy again. . . ."

"See California instead, Lina," I begged.

She looked at us. "I am stronger now than I have been for a while—and February is yet six months away. Perhaps if I am very careful . . . and if I take it easy when I am with you . . ."

"We will see that you do!" Carlo Benedetto seized

her hands. "And you would be a tonic for the Maestro, Lina. If you knew how often he speaks of you."

"Can it be as often as I think of him?" she inquired softly.

"Then you will come, Lina?" I demanded joyfully.

"If we can obtain the consent of your mother. We can do nothing without it. If she trusts me to care for you . . ."

"She will!" I cried. "She must. I'll fetch her." I dashed out of the room. "Mama, Mama . . ."

She emerged from one of the parlors and came half way up the stairs. "Why are you yelling?" she asked sharply.

"Mama, you must let me go! They want me to go. Please, let me go!" I cried.

"Go where?"

"Everywhere!"

"Mrs. Bartlett?" Lina with Carlo Benedetto behind her had come into the hall. "Might we speak to you alone, please?"

Mama nodded. "I think that would be advisable." There was a glint of humor in her blue eyes. "Would you come down here into my office, please." She glanced at me. "You may wait in the hall, Leila."

They were closeted with Mama for what seemed hours while I sat in a chair across from the closed door. I alternated between hope and despair—would Mama allow it or wouldn't she? If only I had not fought with horrid Esau, and if only there had not been that awful business about Victor Davis . . . Until that morning I had believed Mama as interested in my singing as I, but she had said I ought to be married—did she really feel that way or was she only talking? I could not know for sure. Would the door never open? When I was gloomily positive that it never would, it did, and I was summoned inside. As I entered, they all looked at me so gravely that I was sure Mama had refused her permission.

She sat behind her desk and she looked like a judge about to pronounce sentence. She said, "Can I trust you to conduct yourself like a lady and not like a hoyden?"

"Oh, yes, Mama, you can trust me, you truly can!"

She turned to Lina. "Are you sure you want to accompany my daughter?"

"I am sure, Mrs. Bartlett," Lina said.

"Very well," Mama said, "she may go. But remember what you have promised me."

"I shall remember," Lina said.

"And," Mama continued, "if she proves intractable . . ."

"She will be sent home immediately," Carlo Benedetto affirmed. "In chains." He smiled at Mama.

She had no answering smile for him. "I hope I am acting wisely," she sighed.

"Oh, Mama"—tears of happiness stood in my eyes—"you are. You'll never, never regret it, I promise you!"

"I hope not, Leila, I . . ."

Whatever else she had been about to say, I never knew, for I had run around the desk to fling my arms about her rapturously. "Thank you, thank you, thank you!" I practically sang.

I did not think I could live until February 23, which was when we were due to leave for Salt Lake, but there was so much to do that the time passed more quickly than I had expected. I was to sing two roles, Violetta and Nedda; I needed to study them and I needed costumes. These, Mama and I, acting under Lina's instruction, made—I can sew quite well. We also made dresses for everyday and for evening. I had wanted a gown of golden silk with a low décolleté and bugle beads stitched around the V—we compromised on a high neck and no beads.

"You are not a woman of thirty." Mama laughed. "You are only seventeen."

"Eighteen," I had contradicted, "and besides I am an artist—that makes me different."

"Not different, just difficult. And you will remember your promise or . . ."

That was all she needed to say to me. "Oh, Mama," I had cried earnestly, "I do, I will." I am sure that in those months I was more docile, more obedient, than I had ever been in my entire life—not even Esau could unsettle me. In fact, I was absolutely angelic to him—an attitude that appeared to both puzzle and infuriate him. It taught me something about human nature. It was then that I resolved to be as sweet and pleasant as possible, no matter how it irked me inwardly—it would be difficult, but it had its compensations.

Finally, the new horsehair trunk Mama had bought me was packed. My new serge suit, new hat, and new boots were in my closet, while on the dresser were a new pair of gloves and the timetable of the train we were taking on the morrow. I was getting ready for bed, but I knew I would not sleep—I was far too excited. As I brushed my hair, I looked at my reflection in the glass and wondered which of my roles I would sing first. I hoped it would be Violetta, because that would show me off to my public in . . . There was a tap at the door.

"Lina?" I demanded.

"No." Mama entered, frowning. "I want to talk to you." Her tone was so grave it frightened me.

"N-nothing's happened? You—you haven't changed your mind? You couldn't—not at this late date, could you?" I cried.

"No, you may go if you wish," she said, "but I want to tell you about Paulina."

"P-Paulina?" I faltered.

"I've been studying her lately," Mama said. "She's not very well, Leila. Do you think it's fair to uproot her and make her go through all that traveling when . . ."

"She wants to go!" I interrupted. "She's dying to go! Not everybody hates traveling the way you do, Mama!"

"She came here because of her health." Mama continued as if I had not spoken. "She's very fragile . . ."

"She came here because of the air. Signor Benedetto says the air in California is just as good as the air in Denver—better."

"Can't you see beyond your own desires, Leila? Can't you see what you're forcing her to do? You could wait, you know. You're just eighteen . . ."

"Wait!" I cried. "Wait how long? Forever? Why don't you tell the truth, Mama? Why don't you say that you don't think I have a chance to make good—no matter what Carlo Benedetto thinks, though he is more in a position to judge than you! However, no matter what you believe, I shall make good! I shall show you—I shall show everyone that I am a great artist!"

She sighed. "Oh, how you remind me of your father. On and on he went without thinking of me—of you—of his infant son—of anybody except himself."

"I don't understand" I cried. "Why are you telling me this now? Why do you want to spoil everthing for me?"

"You won't see," she said. "Or maybe you can't see, Leila—maybe you're like your father in that, too. I think you must be. I'm afraid for you, I really am."

"I'm not!" I retorted.

"No, I know, and that's your trouble, my dear." She left me then. I sat for a long time, looking into my mirror, but I was not staring at my own image—I was thinking of Lina. Was she too ill? She had seemed much as usual during the last few months. I conjured up a picture of her standing by her piano; she was thin, but she had always been thin, flushed but she was always slightly flushed, and her dark eyes were always circled, too. In fact, she had changed very little in the eight years she had spent with us. What could Mama mean? Jumping to my feet, I hurried down to Lina's room. Tapping on her door, I called, "May I come in?"

"Of course, darling."

She was standing by her window. "There's a lovely moon tonight. So large and yellow—it almost looks like a harvest moon."

I looked at her intently. She did seem thinner. "Are you—are you well?" I faltered. "Are you, Lina?"

"Well?" She stared at me in amazement. "Very well, indeed—and very excited. Why do you ask?"

"I—I shouldn't want you to travel if you didn't want to go," I said.

"Why should you think I didn't want to go, my darling?"

"Mama said . . . she said . . . that I was making you go."

"No one is making me go," she exclaimed. "I want to go, my Leila. To see all my old friends again. The Maestro, oh, you will love the Maestro and he will love you—and we will all be happy at last . . . at long last." She clasped her thin hands. "In the last years, I have been thirsty for my art—and through you I am allowed to drink again!"

"Oh, Lina"—I threw my arms around her—"I love you!"

"And I love you, Leila—you are the child of my heart," she whispered, joyfully. "Now go to bed and do not fret."

I went happily and serenely—well, almost serenely. She had seemed very fragile as I had clasped her—as if in squeezing her too hard, I might have crushed that slender figure. No, that was my imagination. I was sure it was my imagination. Climbing into bed, I was asleep before my head hit the pillow.

Part TWO

Ostensibly, it took thirty hours to cover the 660 miles to Salt Lake. However, to me, the time that stretched between 8:30 A.M. when I bade a tearful farewell to Mama and even to Esau (why I cried, I do not know!) and 3:45 P.M. of the following day seemed *endless!* Much as I was excited by the idea of my first remembered journey, the seats of the car in which Lina and I were ensconced were hard, and there were so many people—at least seventy, each with a wailing child in tow (actually, there were only about three of these but they wailed one at a time, two at a time and then in sympathy with or at each other)—that I thought I should go mad. I said as much to Lina, but she merely remarked that I should get used to it and that I should look out the train window and admire the scenery.

In the years that have passed since that journey, I have often been asked about the rugged beauties of my native state—well, practically my native state since I spent nearly all my youth there—and I have always agreed that the scenery was both rugged and beautiful; but on that particular day, it was also terrifying. It seemed to me that every time I glanced out of the window I was either looking down the jagged sides of a deep gully or up at a towering precipice. It was all very well for the man behind us to comment on the icy whiteness of the glaciers and on the weird shapes of rocks sculptured in the seething cauldrons of some ancient volcano, but he did not have my imagination. He did not see us plunging off the tracks and crashing down a canyon or being crushed by a fall of rock from some overhanging cliff—not an unknown occurence in the mountains; he could look and admire, but if we were to meet such a fate, I did not want to witness it, and consequently, I kept my eyes tightly shut most of the time. Hours later, when we hit the rolling prairies, I found them less monotonous than the other passengers did because they were flat and so was the train. I will not comment on the discomfort of a night spent in an airless upper berth. Truthfully, the thing that impressed me most about our trip was the private railroad car hooked onto the end of our train at Leadville. It belonged, I was told, to a man grown rich on silver mining. One of the boys who sold lemonade and books took time out from his rounds to describe its interior in loving detail. He spoke of silver fittings, leather upholstery, soft beds, a commodious bathroom, kitchen, and bar— complete with a staff of servants, including a French chef and a Chinese valet.

Our seats had grown very hard by this time; we were stiff, tired, and much in need of better food than we could obtain in the dining car. I remarked to Lina, "Wouldn't it be lovely to marry a man with a private railroad car?"

She laughed. "Depending on the man."

"Depending on the money," I said.

"I think you'd need love to go with it, Leila."

"I could learn to love a man with a private railroad car," I sighed.

"You're being childish!" she reproved.

"Why is it childish to want to marry a rich man?"

"Because rich isn't everything," she answered. "Rich isn't strength of character, rich isn't gentleness, kindness, or understanding—and in any relationship, these are the real riches, my dear."

"I don't understand you," I said.

"You will when you are older." She looked at me a long moment, then she added, "I *hope* you will, Leila."

I didn't reply—the train was going around a curve

and I could see the last car with its brightly painted exterior and its curtained windows through which, I was positive, I caught a gleam of silver.

I did not think it would ever happen—but at 3:51¼ by my watch, we rolled into Salt Lake City. There was a large crowd of people on the platform and I am afraid I stared at them with avid curiosity. Though it had been close to sixteen years since polygamy had been abolished in Utah, I was sure that many of the women I saw had lived in harems! Yet, to my mind, they did not look any different than the wholesome, hardy ladies you met on any street corner in Denver— certainly they had nothing in common with the silk-clad maidens I had read about in the *Arabian Nights*. As I scanned the crowds, an ebony cane tapped against my window. Startled, I stared down into the laughing eyes of Carlo Benedetto and forgot completely about harems —we were here, we were really here!

He was waiting at the door as we alighted from the train, and he embraced Lina warmly. *"Carissima,* you have come. I can scarcely believe it, and the Maestro will not credit it, he tells me, until I produce you."

"We are both here, Carlo," she said, pushing me forward.

He smiled at me. "Ah, yes," he said, and then his face changed and he looked at me as if he had never seen me before. "But you are so different!" he exclaimed.

I know I flushed. "You are seeing both of my eyes, perhaps."

"That must be it—and they are green. Or they are gold? I am not sure. I must look more closely." Putting both hands on my shoulders, he stared into them. "I still cannot tell," he complained.

"You will have other opportunities to find out, my dear," Lina said. "Meanwhile, we must attend to our luggage."

He moved back from me immediately, and as he took his hands from my shoulders, I discovered that

I had liked his touch—liked, too, his dark eyes fixed on mine. It had made me feel . . . I could not define how it had made me feel. I did not have time to think about it because we needed to get our trunks, and then there was the business of arranging for them to be sent to the accomodations Carlo had reserved for us. He took care of everything for us and presently we were seated in a carriage—horsed, not horseless, for which I was thankful; I could not have borne the jolting, the wheezing, the groaning, and the dust that was part of every automobile ride.

"Shall we hear the opera tonight?" I demanded.

"Tonight?" Lina echoed, closing her eyes wearily and leaning back in her seat.

Carlo shook his head. "We are not playing tonight—that which we choose to call a theater has been pre-empted for a lecture on the Holy Land by a recently returned Saint."

"A—Saint?" I questioned.

"The elders of the Mormon Church are all called Saints," he explained.

"Oh," I said. "If we are not to hear the opera tonight, what are we to do?"

"Do?" Lina sighed. "I will rest and so should you, my dear. I presume the Maestro will want to hear you tomorrow. Isn't that true, Carlo?"

"Tomorrow at eleven," he corroborated. "You should rest, but if you would like to see a few sights of this town, perhaps I might show you some of them before I return to my hotel."

I clasped my hands. "Would you? I should like it about all things!"

Carlo turned to Lina. "I shan't keep her out long," he said.

She hesitated. "Remember, too, that I am her chaperon."

An amused glint appeared in his eyes. "Do you not trust me, Lina?" he inquired softly.

She smiled. "I do, but would Mrs. Bartlett allow her

daughter to go walking in a strange city with a young man . . ."

"A young man," he repeated. "I am old enough to be her—her . . ."

"Uncle," Lina supplied with a laugh. "I can grant you no more than that, dear Carlo."

"Uncle, brother, or cousin," he said lightly, "I can be trusted with this child."

"Child again!" I pouted. "Why do you persist in calling me a child when you know that I am now eighteen!"

"And I am more than a decade older than that—which should satisfy both mothers and chaperons."

"Please, Lina," I begged; I should love to visit a harem!"

They looked at each other and laughed, then Lina said, "Very well, Carlo, you have my sanction."

I almost clapped my hands but remembered just in time that it was childish, so I kept them folded in my lap and tried to look as dignified as I could for the remainder of the ride.

I had hoped we would stay at a hotel, but Carlo had secured us a room in a large old house similar to Mama's. However, it was clean and neat and we overlooked a garden. It was furnished with a large clothes press, two beds side by side, and two dressers each topped by a china ewer and basin.

As I poured water into the basin preparatory to washing my face and hands, Lina sank down on a rocking chair near the window and smiled at me wearily. "I wish I had your stamina. Oh, Leila, you are so lucky—do you know it? You are talented, beautiful, and healthy. You will have the whole world at your feet one day and you will be able to keep it there—you'll not have to stop in the middle of your life!"

I stared at her reflection in the mirror over my dresser and I felt a little twinge of panic. Was it the uneven glass that made her look so pale, so fragile? I ran to her and knelt beside her chair.

"Lina, think that I am you—think that you have not stopped but are continuing through me. I would be nothing without you and you know it." In that moment, I actually felt that there was indeed very little of me in me—that in some strange way I was only a receptacle for Paulina's soul. It was an odd, frightening realization. It made me uncomfortable and unhappy.

She took my face between her hands and looked into my eyes. "No, Leila, you are you," she said, "but I shall treasure our words and be the richer for them. You are growing up, child and I see the artist emerging, the real artist. I am very happy for that."

I did not understand her words, but I felt the better for them. Still, I did not want to leave her. "I shan't go out this afternoon, Lina—I'll stay with you."

"No," she said. "I only want to rest—go and have a good time, but don't tire yourself too much. Remember, tomorrow you'll sing for the Maestro, who is very critical, and there may be others listening who are even more critical, though with less cause."

"What others?"

"Members of the company. But do not think about them now. Go down to Carlo. I am sure he will grow impatient if you keep him waiting much longer."

He was standing in the hall as I came down the stairs, and since he was turned a little away from me, I had a chance to observe him before he saw me. For once, he was not smiling, and in repose, his face was somber and a little sad. Yet he was, I decided with a little thrill of surprise, quite handsome. It was a pity he was not taller—all the men I had admired were tall and muscular—but he was delicately built, slim of body, slender of hands and feet, and . . . My scrutiny ended as he turned toward me. He raised his eyebrows. "What have you done to yourself?" he demanded. "You look as fresh and glowing as tomorrow morning."

"I only washed my face," I said, running down the rest of the stairs.

He looked into my eyes. "Green," he said.

"My face?"

"Your eyes, little one. Do not be coy. You understood me." He opened the door. "Come, before it grows too late to see this glorious mecca for Mormons."

"You don't like it?" I asked.

He shrugged. "I have no feelings of like or dislike. It is a town like many towns across this great country."

"What is your favorite town in the whole world?" I asked.

"In the whole world?" He smiled. "You make it sound so vast, the world—it is not, you know. It is a small planet and growing even smaller. But you do not wish to talk of such things. You wish to see the Lion House, which is your harem, and the Beehive—they are not far from here. They are on South Temple Street, and then, if you are not tired, I shall show you the Salt Palace.

"Is it made of salt?"

"It is covered with rock-salt crystals and illuminated by electricity—it is most monstrously ugly. Perhaps you would like to see it first?"

"No," I said. "The Lion House first."

Though he was, at the most, an inch taller than I, I still had trouble keeping up with him as we walked, and I was panting slightly by the time we stood in front of one of the strangest houses I had ever seen. It had twenty gables! "Do you suppose each one of those sheltered a wife?"

"So they say," he replied. "But Brigham Young had twenty-six wives, poor man."

"I think he was horrid!" I said hotly. "Those *poor* women—and he called himself a saint!"

"Only a saint could put up with twenty-six women," Carlo answered.

"You don't like women?" I inquired.

"Would you like twenty-six husbands?" he countered.

"If they all had private railroad cars, I might."

"Private railroad cars?" he echoed. "You would have an entire train! Do you have such a passion for traveling?"

"In style," I said, and told him about the man from Leadville.

He frowned. "So you are ambitious as well as talented. Is your art to be used as a ladder to social success? Is that why you are so eager to sing?"

"No!" I exclaimed. "I love to sing."

His frown remained. "Is that the truth or do you believe I wish to hear such a truth from you? Am I to suspect you of slyness, little one?"

"It's the truth," I assured him, wondering at the anger that had flared in his eyes and at the sadness that lingered after it was gone.

"For your sake, I hope so. You have a great talent. It should not be wasted. Yet, will you be able to withstand the temptations or will you end up singing at tea parties?"

"Tea parties!" I exclaimed, horrified.

His laughter filled the air. "That is the sort of answer I like. Come—we will go to the Beehive and the Salt Palace, then I shall take you back to Line."

Our walk ended far too soon for me. After he left me in the hall, I sped to a window to watch him. He moved very gracefully. While I had been with him, I had not noticed his grace or his elegance. All too quickly, he turned a corner and vanished from my sight. I wished he had looked back. Of course, he could not know I was watching to catch one more glimpse of a face I had already memorized feature by feature, yet wanted to see again. Sighing, I went upstairs. I should have liked to ask Lina more about Carlo, but when I came in, she was already asleep.

Lina and I arrived at the theater at half-past ten the following morning. It was not what I had expected—it was on the second floor of an old wooden building and looked more like a lecture hall than a theater. The seats were all on one level and the stage was very shallow. However, I did notice a canvas backdrop depicting a garden scene, and below the stage were a number of music stands and chairs, suggesting the eventual arrival of an orchestra. There was also a piano shoved into one corner. I wondered if Carlo would play for me, then heard his laugh. Turning, I saw him come in with a slender dark girl, swathed in furs. She clung tightly to his arm, smiling at him in a manner that infuriated me, though I could not have said why. Lina had looked back, too, and her figure grew curiously rigid.

"Helena," she murmured.

"Paulina, is it possible!" The girl with Carlo dropped his arm and ran lightly down the aisle. "My dearest, darling Lina, who disappeared in the great American desert never to be heard of again. If you only knew how often I have asked for you—and Carlo, the bad boy, never told me until this morning that you are here with the child who is to sing. And this is she?" She had spoken quickly, almost breathlessly, in a voice I found almost sickeningly sweet. Facing me, she smiled warmly but eyed me coldly. "Oh, the precious, precious lamb, so young, so very young. Carlo, *carissimo,* you told me she was the merest baby, but I did not believe you until now—so many times you exaggerate."

Lina's manner toward her was curiously repressed. "She is young, Helena, but I assure you she is a mature artist, as you will soon hear for yourself. Leila, my dear, this is Helena Montoya—and this Helena, is Leila MacKenzie."

"Charmed!" she exclaimed.

I inclined my head. "I am delighted to meet you," I said in a tone cool enough to contradict my words. Having disliked her at a distance, naturally she had proved no more enchanting at close proximity. Furthermore, I was positive that she also hated me. Then, quite innocently, I said the thing that provoked even more animosity. "Are you a singer too?"

Her forced smile faded. "Too?" she said between her teeth. "Yes, I am a singer too."

"Madame Montoya is leaving the company to fulfill a contract with the Chicago Opera," Carlo said quickly.

"Oh, you're leaving!" I am afraid I sounded as relieved as I felt.

She nodded curtly and looked anxiously at Carlo. "I

had been going with a clear conscience, *caro,* but now—to replace me with one so young and so clearly inexperienced . . . I suppose you could make do with Antonia, though her voice is heavy for Violetta . . . Clara's coloratura is, on the other hand, a trifle light and . . ."

"I can sing . . ." I began, and stopped as I met her eyes and knew she was deliberately goading me. I drew a deep breath, but before I could have answered her as I should have liked, Lina said quickly, "Ah, there is the Maestro!"

As lightly as Helena Montoya had run to us, she sped to meet the frail, elderly man who had appeared at the entrance. Taller than Carlo, he had similar features. He put out a beautifully shaped, paper-white hand. It trembled a little, but his grasp as he seized Lina was firm and his voice deep and sonorous when he said emotionally, *"Cara, bellissima* Lina!" Enfolding her in his arms, he added, "I did not think I should live to see you again, but now that I do, I am young again!"

"It is a pity that Lina cannot sing for you, Carlo," Helena Montoya remarked in low but purposely audible tones. "She was always a lovely Violetta, but I can see it is not possible, poor woman. Such a change!"

I opened my mouth, but again I was thwarted as Carlo, placing his hand beneath my elbow, firmly guided me toward the Maestro, saying, "I want you to meet my father." He whispered, "Angry words will not serve your purpose. Sing for me as well as you sang for me that day in the studio and you will have all the revenge you covet."

"But . . . " I started to say.

"Shhhhh," he cautioned. "Do as I say."

I could make no further protest, for we had reached the Maestro and Lina, and the old man was looking at me with interest and, I thought, some doubt. Predictably, he said, "But she is so very young."

"Isn't she, Maestro?" Helena had come up behind us. "A mere baby. They will call it immoral, the papers, if such a child sings the role of a courtesan."

"I can look older," I said. "It's easier to look older than younger, I should think." I let my eyes rest on Helena's face and was rewarded by her venomous glare and the Maestro's laughter.

"Miss MacKenzie is quite right," he approved. "Youth can ape age, but age is always at a disadvantage —except behind the footlights, where there is magic at work. But we must hear you, Miss MacKenzie. Are you ready?"

I had been more than ready until he questioned me, then suddenly I was so nervous that my knees were shaking. I looked wildly from him to Lina, then I caught Helena's measuring glance and I was positive she could see into my mind. I said, "Yes, I am, Maestro Benedetto."

I walked steadily down the aisle again and up onto the stage. Carlo followed me, and pushing the piano out from its niche, he sat down, running his fingers lightly over the keys. I looked at him, saw his slight nod. I looked at the Maestro, sitting with Lina at the back of the hall, then I saw Helena Montoya at the front—in the second row. Her expression was mocking—it seemed to question my right to be on the stage. "Too young, too young, too young," it jeered. I would show her, I thought. Then I heard the music. Carlo was playing "Ah fors'è lui." I glanced at him, then I understood Violetta as I never had before. She had seen a man she could love. Would he bring her the happiness that had always eluded her?" Or would she only be disappointed again? But she was born to be disappointed, deluded—she could not trust her own feelings, or the men that pursued her. I envisioned Helena hanging onto Carlo's arm and I knew what that meant, too—but it did not matter because I was young and I was free, always free—*sempre libera!* I was hardly aware when the last notes of the music died away. I was exultant! There was clapping in the hall, and the Maestro was at my side. His eyes gleamed. "My dear ... " He shook his head. "But I have seldom heard anything like it. Seldom!"

When I try to remember exactly what happened after that, I am never sure—Lina spoke to me and Carlo; I was introduced to other people in the hall, members of the Benedetto Troupe, none of whom I recalled when we met again. There was laughter and applause, and an elderly lady who wept and said, "She is so young, how lovely!" I already had my contract, but I would probably sing more performances than those assigned me—it would depend on my debut, which would take place in the middle of the following week. In Sacramento, I would sing my first Nedda, meanwhile I would have blocking rehearsals with Carlo, my conductor. All in all it was a most momentous occasion. As Lina said later, I had come and I had conquered, and as a final celebration, there was a champagne supper at the hotel where Carlo and his father were staying. Just the four of us were there, and I am afraid I grew a little lightheaded on the champagne because I have only a hazy memory of being driven back to our lodgings and no memory at all of writing the name "Carlo" in the journal I had decided to keep when we started on our trip—but it was there the next morning, sprawled across one whole page and underscored heavily. I blushed when I looked at it, and felt—well, I did not know quite what I felt, except that I was looking forward to those rehearsals!

Three days later, the pages of that same journal were tear-stained and one of them had been torn across—I had crumpled that half and thrown it into the wastebasket. It would never do for anyone to see that I had written, *"She* always waits for him. I *hate* them *both!"*

She was Olivia Seton, the vivacious blonde mezzo-soprano who would sing Flora to my Violetta; she also sang Maddalena in *Rigoletto*, Lola in *Cavalleria Rusticana*, and La Cieca in *La Gioconda*. She was considered very pretty by the men in the company, but though she laughed and joked with them, she was interested in only one man, and as far as I could tell, he was equally interested in her. The rehearsals to which I had looked forward with such high hopes were only hours of work —learning where to move and becoming accustomed to the vagaries of my colleagues, the baritone, Mario Rampolo and the tenor, Jacomo Rignoli. Both of these gentlemen seemed to loathe me on sight, especially the tenor, who made faces at me during our love duets, tried to drown out my high notes, and invariably turned away from me so that if I faced him, I would be singing upstage or into the wings. These, however, were minor problems, for Lina, who watched me work, had tricks of her own to teach me. Would she could have helped me foil Olivia Seton! However, she knew nothing about my hopeless passion for Carlo Benedetto because I did not mention my woes—I confided in no one until the afternoon of my first stage rehearsal.

The first act had gone reasonably well; so had the second, but in the third act, I could not seem to please Carlo, who kept stopping the orchestra to yell at me, "You are so stiff—you move like a wax doll. Try it again!" Finally—the fourth time he stopped the music— he said, "Watch Olivia. See how freely she moves in her scenes. Why can't you do the same?"

It was too much—to be reprimanded and to be compared unfavorably to that woman, who was looking at me with a smile in which I read only odious triumph! I burst into tears, and a number of chorus ladies surrounded me, all murmuring and patting my shoulder.

"Enough!" Carlo exploded. "She is not a child. She is supposedly a professional singer and we do not have the time for tears. Leave the stage at once, and as for you, Miss MacKenzie, if you cannot control your emotions, you have no place here!"

I heard a snicker behind me; whirling, I saw Rignoli's eyes. They were bright with malice. With a chilling certainty, I knew he wanted me to fail. I would show him. Angrily, I brushed my hand across my eyes. "I am sorry, Maestro," I said. "I will try it again." Much to my relief, he did not stop the orchestra again and I knew that the fourth act went very well. When we were dismissed, however, I hurried off the stage, wanting to get out of the hall as soon as possible. I was stopped at the door by Antonia Valdi, the soprano who sang the dramatic roles.

"My dear," she said quickly, "Lina could not come and she asked if I would watch for you and take you home."

Her words only made me more miserable. Every day after rehearsal, I went back with Lina to our lodgings. I was not allowed to mix with the members of the troupe. That had been the promise Mama had exacted from Lina and she had abided by it—strictly. I hardly knew anyone. "I—I do not need to—to be—taken h-home," I half sobbed. "I—I—can find my way."

"But I want to talk to you," she said gently. "I saw the rehearsal. Lina wanted me to watch it."

I flushed. "Please don't tell her about . . ." I began, then I sighed. "But Carlo will tell her, he'll say I am not p-professional."

"Child"—she put her arm around me—"come, we will go to my rooms at the hotel and we will have hot chocolate and a little talk, yes? I should like to speak to you about Carlo—I think you must know about him and then you will no longer be affronted. He does not castigate you—it is someone else he scolds."

"I do not understand."

"I can help you to understand," she said.

The suite of rooms Antonia and her husband, Rinaldo Valdi—the concertmaster of the orchestra—occupied in the Hotel Zion bore evidence of a domesticity I had not expected to find in the habitat of a prima donna! The hard horsehair chairs and sofas provided by the management were draped with antimacassars of her own making; a large bag in the corner contained knitting needles and half a shawl; and on every table there were photographs of two children, a boy and a girl. She saw me looking at them, and with a mixture of sadness and pride, she said, "Those are our two children, Rosa and Tonio—she is six and he is eleven. They are with my parents in Genoa—we shall see them in three more months. I can hardly wait. It has been such a long time that I am afraid they will forget me."

"Can't they travel with you?"

She shook her head. "The road is no life for a child, especially in the American West, where you are never sure what accomodations you will have. Sometimes you are stranded at train stations in the cold, sometimes the train does not come at all. No, it is better that they have always the same house and the same garden in which to play. But sit down. I shall heat the milk for the chocolate."

Casting her cloak aside, she bustled out of the room, leaving me a trifle pensive. Evidently the road did not have the same charms for everyone who traveled it. Yet Antonia Valdi was a fine artist with a superb voice—Lina had told me so. Audiences were at her feet wherever she sang, but obviously she was not as happy as she might have been. I shivered slightly. Would there come a time when I would be lonely, when the cheers of an audience would not be enough for me? I looked at the pictures. I could not ever imagine having a child of my own, and yet—Carlo's face rose before my eyes. Angrily, I banished it. I did not want to think about him—or Olivia Seton!

Antonia came back. "Take off your coat," she ordered. "You will be far too warm in here—all the windows are closed. I like the air, myself, but Rinaldo does not, and he is resting in the other room. The chocolate will be ready in a minute." She put my coat in a closet. "You did beautifully today, you know. I was amused to see that you did not allow Rignoli to trick you into hiding your face—Lina has taught you well and you are a good pupil. Also you are a fine singer, and the combination has put poor Carlo on his mettle—on his guard, too. Obviously, he is afraid of you."

"Afraid of *me*?" I repeated, incredulously.

She nodded, then she frowned. "No, I did not put that quite correctly—he is afraid of himself, poor Carlo. He has a good heart, a big heart, and he does not want to have it broken again, so he guards himself carefully and punishes you for what he fears will happen when they come."

"They?"

"The big impresarios from New York and Chicago with the contracts, the very tempting contracts for you. He looks ahead to San Francisco and he sees them in the audience and he sees you leaving us as she did, three years ago. It took him a long time to get over that." She sighed. "Poor Carlo."

"She?" I prompted.

"Wait, I will get our chocolate." She rose and left the room, while I ground my teeth in impatience, wondering who *she* was.

A moment later, she was back with a tray on which reposed an ornate silver teapot, obviously an heirloom, and some heavy china mugs; there was also a plate of cookies. "Try the white ones," she said. "I baked them this morning and I think they are the best."

"You cook and everything?" I demanded.

"Oh, yes," she replied. "I cannot abide hotel food and nor can Rinaldo—he does the cooking on the nights I sing. Sometimes when neither of us are performing, you and Lina must come to dinner. Often Carlo comes with the Maestro—he does not have many home-cooked meals, poor boy. It is a pity he did not marry his Carola. He needs a wife, though probably she would not have made him as happy as he imagined."

"Who was Carola?" I asked.

"She is Carola Cartieri," Antonia laughed. "Carol Carter, if the truth were known—her mother thought Carola Cartieri sounded more Italian."

"Carola Cartieri!" I repeated. "But I have heard of her. She made her debut at the Metropolitan Opera two seasons ago. She was with you?"

"In New England. It was in Boston that Conreid heard her. She was much on your type, slim, fair, young —not as young as you, but beautiful and with a beautiful voice. It was, I believe, love at first sight with Carlo and with Carola, too, but her mother was ambitious and she tried to keep them apart. She was not entirely successful. I am of the opinion that if Conreid had not made his offer . . . But he did and Carola left. The tragedy of it was that Carlo could have gone with her, because Conreid wanted him—but he cannot leave the Maestro, who depends on him for everything."

"He never heard from Carola afterward?" I asked.

"Last year, she was married to a cousin of the Astors."

I had a sudden memory of my walk with Carlo on the day of my arrival. "A private railroad car," I whispered.

"What?" she demanded, staring at me.

"She must be very rich, now," I said.

"Very," she agreed. "Though often I have wondered if she is happy. In her pictures, she does not look as happy as when she was with us."

The happiness of Carola Cartieri was not one of my concerns. I was pondering her words and wondering if I had interpreted them correctly. Hesitantly, I said, "You are saying that—that Carlo might like *me?*"

She gave me a long searching look. "I think he likes you a great deal. And you, do you like Carlo?" Her look grew even more intent. "I see you do. . . . It is in your eyes and in your flushed cheeks. I do not mean to embarrass you, my dear, but I am glad to have had this talk with you. I want you to understand him."

"But there is Olivia Seton!" I cried.

"Olivia!" She snapped her fingers. "She is nothing to him. Carlo is not a man to be pursued—he comes to you, you do not go to him. In that, he is like all the men in the world—they do not want what they can have easily." Her eyes grew somber. "If you do like Carlo, be kind to him, but . . . You are so very young, and soon there will be so many men to court you—I think Carlo does well to stay away from you."

"No!" I cried. "I—I . . ." I looked down. The memory of the last three days was large in my mind. Even given his reasons, I could not entirely forgive him for his uncompromising attitude. I was not prepared to tell her I loved him, nor was I sure I did. My conflicting emotions must have been very apparent to her, for she put a gentle hand on my arm.

"Do not waste too much time suffering over Carlo," she advised. "You have your debut to think about and that should take precedence over all. Remember, strong emotions are well enough to simulate on stage, but they are not good for the voice."

"Aren't they? Why not?"

"Because they cause tensions and we must be free—as your Violetta says, *"Sempre libera."* She patted my shoulder. "You will be a lovely Violetta, my dear. You've nothing to worry about. Not even contumacious conductors can keep you from being a success."

"Oh, Antonia," I said, "why are you so different from all the others? You are so kind!"

She laughed at me. "Perhaps I would not be so kind if you were in my voice category. One day you will be, and then I shall pass you with my nose in the air!"

"I don't believe it." I laughed back.

"No, do not believe it. I am secure in myself and in my art. I need not envy anyone. I envy only those women who have their children by their side." She sighed. "Art is a terrible master. Always you must give up much for it—sometimes too much. But you never think about that until it is too late." She shivered slightly. "I am talking too much. I do not want to frighten you."

"I am not frightened." I rose. "But I am grateful you spoke to me. Thank you, too, for the chocolate. I had better get back to my lodgings."

"I will walk with you," she said. "Lina would not want you to go alone."

"But it's not far," I protested.

"All the same, I made a promise to Lina. I do not want to worry her unduly—she is not very well. I think she should not have come with you."

"She wanted to come," I said defensively. "You saw how happy she was to be with the Maestro—with all of you—again."

A Shadow on the House   57

She still continued to look grave. "She is headstrong. She sang long beyond the time when she should have, and collapsed in the wings one night. They had to ring down the curtain and send the audience home."

"She never told me about that."

"She never would. She does not speak of her sorrows, nor does she complain much of her health—but do not let her do too much, my dear. She is not strong."

"Oh, I shan't!" I cried, feeling very guilty. "I shall be very careful of her . . . ."

Antonia left me at my door. "No, I shan't come in," she said. "I must get back to Rinaldo. He will be practicing and will want me to hear his violin solo of Act III. We criticize each other, you know."

I stood for a moment watching her hurry down the street. It seemed an ideal relationship, a singer and a concertmaster. Yet, they were not very wealthy. You would think that an artist of Antonia's accomplishments could have the world, but perhaps she had married before she had become successful. I let my mind stray to Carola Cartieri, who had wed an Astor cousin, and then the door behind me opened and Carlo appeared on the threshold; he was grave and unsmiling. "I have been waiting for you," he said abruptly. "Come into the parlor." Grasping my wrist, he led me inside.

At his touch, at his presence, all thoughts of anything else vanished and I followed him dutifully into the parlor, which was fortunately unoccupied. He sat opposite me and it seemed to me that his gaze was stern. It frightened me, or something did, for my heart was pounding. His first words were not what I had expected.

"Take your coat off," he ordered, and getting up, he helped me divest myself of it. "You do not want to catch a cold."

His inadvertant touch on my shoulder stirred more fugitive pulses. "Thank you," I said.

He nodded curtly, sitting down opposite me again. "You are no doubt wondering why I have been as I have been these last few days," he said abruptly.

"No," I began, thinking of Antonia's explanation but

immediately guessing he would not want me to know it. "I mean—yes," I stuttered, feeling foolish.

A glint of amusement shone in his eyes, vanishing in a second. "It is not to be expected that you would know when I myself am not sure. It is only that I think I expect too much. You are doing very well, Leila—to do any better than you are doing, you would have to be older and wiser and that would be to lose the quality you now possess. You are very vulnerable and I think Violetta might have been vulnerable, too. She was young, too—so you must not worry or think yourself unprepared. Lina has done an excellent job."

"Oh," I drew a long breath. "Thank you. I thought you must have come to scold me."

He frowned. "Have I become such an ogre to you?"

"No, only . . . "

"I have not meant to be an ogre," he said gently. "But I warn you, you will find many like me who are difficult in the pit, worse even than I. So far, everything has been very easy for you, Leila—too easy, I think. Perhaps that is why I have been hard on you." He looked puzzled, and more to himself he repeated, "Yes, I think that might be the explanation." He rose quickly. "I must go now."

I felt a twinge of disappointment. I wanted—I was not sure what I wanted. Was it the camaraderie I had experienced that first day in Salt Lake or was it something more? I thought of Carola Cartieri and suddenly she was almost a palpable presence—standing between us. I hated her.

"Why are you looking so fierce?" he demanded. "Are you still angry with me?"

My cheeks grew warm. "I am not angry with you," I said.

"Good." He pressed my hand. "I hope we understand each other. Do we?"

"Yes, Carlo, and thank you." I managed a friendly smile, even though my lips were unaccountably stiff.

He was still holding my hand and he moved closer

to me, looking into my eyes. Then, shaking his head, he said, "You must not thank me, my dear, you deserved an explanation." I had the feeling he wanted to say more, but he did not—he only bowed, muttered a farewell, and strode from the room. As I had that first day, I watched him from the window, hoping that this time he would look back; but he didn't.

On the night of March 7th, I stood on stage staring at the canvas curtain and noticing that it was patched in places and that it had a large stain a little to the left of center. I was also aware of the continuous whispering of the chorus members, poised in their places, holding glasses of the weak tea that was supposed to be champagne. Bits of their conversation reached me. They talked of Sunday outings, of their homes in various parts of the country, of their children, of anything except the forthcoming ordeal, but of course, it was no ordeal for them—they had sung the same music night after night and sung it together. They were comfortable in their shabby gowns and shiny suits—they did not have new shoes that pinched, they did not have to manage a costume they had worn only once before. I moved restively and the crinoline bounced slightly. It was an odd feeling. I did not want to think about it. I shot a glance toward the wings and saw Lina standing there, her hand resting on a pole— no it was not resting, it was clutching the pole. She was tense, worried about me. Behind her stood the Maestro; was he, too, worried? I looked away from them and met the eyes of Rignoli, looking young and oddly handsome in his stage makeup. His expression should have been ardent, but as usual it was malicious. I looked away quickly and saw Olivia Seton in a rich scarlet gown. She smiled at me; it was not a nice smile. I stared down at the floor—the floor was safer. I did not want to think about her or about any of them. I had other problems, mainly my tongue—it was frozen and lay behind my teeth like a piece of marble; and if that were not enough, I could not remember my first line—and even if I did remember it, I could not sing it since I was unable to move my marble tongue. Meanwhile, behind or rather in front of that lowered curtain, I heard strange rustling noises. There were people out there, waiting to be entertained. By me? Why was I there? I had no business being there! I should like to be back on the train. I would rather be looking at those yawning caverns than standing here under a cardboard chandelier, in front of a backdrop painted with pillars and velvet hangings, amidst all these unfriendly people. The music had begun; panic swept through me—soon, soon, I should have to sing, but I could not sing. I tried to move my tongue. I could not even wiggle it! I cast a terrified glance toward the wings and met Lina's eyes. I could not run to her; she would thrust me back, and besides I could not move. Something had happened! The curtain had vanished and I was looking down into the pit, into Carlo's face; his baton was lifted and behind me the chorus was singing and Olivia was surging toward me with a gallant on either arm—Gaston and Alfredo! There was something in my hand. It was a wine glass. I had forgotten it was there. Why was it there? Familiar music was in my ears. My mouth stretched back in a smile. I looked at dear Flora, my friend.

"Flora, amici . . ." I cried with my suddenly lively tongue, and amazingly, my voice was loud in my ears, carried along by the music, by Carlo in the pit. I can compare my sensations only to swimming—I was swimming in a sea of melody and I could not resist that strong current. Suddenly, I was very, very happy—suddenly, I was enjoying myself as I never had in all my life!

It went well—very well. I know that because everyone told me it did, but the specifics are lost. I cannot remember how I sang—I only know that I did, act after act, until I was lying on the floor with Rignoli crouching beside me uttering musical moans while Rampolo sobbed overhead. Then the curtain thudded to the floor and my colleagues, both grinning broadly, pulled me to my feet. I needed their support. I literally hung between them as the curtain rose and fell again and again to that most welcome of all sounds in the world—applause. Afterward, there were flowers—two enormous baskets and a smaller bouquet of camelias, one of which I kept and pressed between the pages of my journal because it had been given to me by Carlo. He had come out of the pit to take a bow with the cast, but he had not come with me to my dressing room. Only the Maestro and Lina had accompanied me—they and a bevy of strangers in evening dress, men and women, all talking at once. I was introduced to several of them. I smiled, I spoke, I do not know what I said or what they said to me—I was still in a daze. I think the Maestro kissed me and held my hands. After he left me, Lina also kissed me and then, with the aid of the wardrobe lady, helped me out of my costume—but I was hardly conscious of these ministrations or of my surroundings until after I had slipped into my golden evening gown. With the return of my equilibrium came a feeling of hunger. I had been unable to eat before the performance, but now I was ravenous and we had been invited to have supper at the Maestro's suite in the hotel. I was eager to go, but much against my will, Lina made me remain in my dressing room. "We must wait."

"Why?" I demanded mutinously. "I am famished!"

She laughed. "You won't starve, I promise you. It is customary to wait. We will go in good time and you will make a grand entrance. Then, I promise you, you will be glad you waited."

I sat down and then I jumped up. "Oh, I can't stay in here!" I cried. "I want to walk—I want to feel the wind on my face. Couldn't I walk around the block, Lina?"

"In this weather!" She looked horrified. "It is not

spring yet and the wind is chill. You must take care of your throat, my dear."

"At least let me have a breath of fresh air," I exclaimed. "It's stifling in here!" Whirling away from her, I pulled open my door and started out, crashing into Carlo, who was standing just outside. "Oh," I gasped, clutching at him; "did I hurt you?"

His arms had gone around me. He held me tightly against his chest for a single instant. "No," he said softly, "you did not hurt me, my Leila." He released me hastily, all too hastily, and moving around me, he went to Lina and bowed over her hand. "Are you ready?" he demanded.

"Yes, we're ready." She looked at me. "More than ready."

"Then," he said gaily, "let us be off!"

"Carlo!" I cried. "Did you like my singing? Did I do well?"

"But have I not told you so?" he demanded.

"You told me nothing!" I pouted.

"He did, darling," Lina said. "When you came off the stage."

"You d-d-d-did?" I stuttered, feeling guilty for some reason. "I—didn't hear you."

He laughed a little harshly. "Spoken like a true prima donna!" he said.

I did not understand his laughter but it hurt me. I felt as if a barrier of some sort had been erected between us; but the carriage bore us toward the hotel, I thought it might have been my imagination, for his arm was around me and he laughed often and seemed as happy as I over the success of my debut.

When we entered the Maestro's suite, I understood why Lina had made me wait. People had been standing around talking or drinking, but when I came in, a sudden silence fell, and again I heard the lovely sound of applause—this time from my colleagues. Then Rignoli came forward, glass in hand. For once there was no trace of malice in his glance as he said, "Here is to the prima donna!"

"To the prima donna," Carlo echoed. "I'll drink to that."

"To the prima donna!" everyone chorused.

I looked about me ecstatically. I was completely happy. I had arrived!

Part
THREE

It is amazing how quickly the unusual becomes the usual, especially when you are vaguely dissatisfied and unhappy, as I was after my success. On reading what I have written thus far, I think I might have lavished too many words on that early period, yet for my own elucidation it has been necessary, especially if I am going to understand what happened to me when I came to California and into the situation that so nearly altered the course of my life.

They say there are mystics who are capable of reading the future. Would that I might have known one of these people in the days before I went to the house that was known as the Casa d'oro—at least officially—because I might have been forearmed against what happened; but if my palm had been read or a crystal scryed for me, I think I would have laughed at the forecast and deemed it fanciful, for in those days, I could think of little beyond the phrase "San Francisco in the spring." It was something that the whole company repeated like a litany.

San Francisco in the spring meant the conclusion of the tour, though it also meant hard work since two new operas were to be added—*Lucia di Lammermoor* and *La Sonambula,* both vehicles for the remarkable Rosa Feranti, who would join us in Stockton, where rehearsals would begin. Furthermore, we would be seeing what Antonia termed one of the most picturesque cities in the world—a blend of old Spain, old China, and new America near the Golden Gate, surely one of the most beautiful harbors in the world. For me, who had never seen an ocean except in photographs, the prospect was particularly exciting. Then, too, I should not only be singing Violetta but I would be performing Nedda. The twin bill of *Pagliacci* and *Cavalleria Rusticana*—*Cav* and *Pag,* we called it—would be unveiled in Sacramento. I would sing two performances of *Traviata* there—one on the second night after our arrival; I would also sing two Neddas, and I would have four more of the same in Stockton and in San Francisco. Lina was delighted and I should have been perfectly happy—but I was not, for Carlo remained aloof.

In fact, his attitude was so impersonal that I could almost believe the moment when he had held me so tightly had never occurred. Yet, occasionally, I would catch him looking at me with an odd brooding expression that vanished the minute he caught my eye. I was at a loss to account for his behavior—well, not entirely at a loss, for I remembered his remark of my debut night: "Spoken like a true prima donna!" Could he hold it against me that in my excitement I had been unaware of him? Had it hurt his feelings? Was he equating me with Carola Cartieri? It hardly seemed right to blame me for anything that had happened that night! But perhaps he did, and if he did, he was being totally unfair! He knew what it was to perform—he knew, he knew! I had seen him step down from the podium in just as dazed a condition as mine that night—so why? Why? These were the thoughts that tormented me in the hours I was not rehearsing or practicing Nedda with Lina. I was alternately torn and unhappy, excited and ecstatic! In other words, I was full of myself to the exclusion of everything and everybody. I can see that now, but I couldn't then. Oh, if I had only been just a little more perceptive!

We left Salt Lake City on Sunday, March 11th. It was 781 miles to Sacramento and it took us thirty-two hours by train. This time, Lina and I shared a private compartment, and when we had taken possession of it, I had been pleased by the knowledge that the

Benedettos were only two doors away from us. Surely, since both father and son were so fond of Lina, they would visit us and I should be able to engage Carlo's attention. However, there was no sign of them in the hours preceding lunchtime, and when Lina and I made our way into the dining car, we discovered Carlo and Olivia sharing a table with Antonia and Rinaldo! I need not add that I ate very little—indeed, I could scarcely wait to get back to our compartment. Once inside, I burst into tears.

"Darling, whatever's the matter?" Lina asked anxiously.

"C-C-Carlo. I—I h-hate h-him and that . . . that h-horrid woman, the—the way he—he l-looks at—at her and she—she's always smiling and . . . " For the first time I confided everything to Lina.

She listened in silence, and when I had concluded what proved a lengthy catalogue, she put her arm around me, saying gently and much to my annoyance, tolerantly, "But all young sopranos fall in love with conductors and fall out of love as easily. You wait, my dear."

I looked at her incredulously. "You . . . you think it—it's only a p-passing—f-fancy with me? But it's not. I—I've never f-felt this way about anyone before—none of the boys at—at home . . . "

"None of the boys at home were like Carlo—it's because he's so different that you think you love him."

"It's n-not!" I sobbed. "And—and he liked me, too. Oh, what did I do to make him—h-hate me?"

"Leila, he doesn't hate you. He's very fond of you!"

"F-fond!" I howled. "You are f-fond of a d-dog. I want him to love me!"

"No, you don't," Lina said firmly, "because no good would come of it. It would be madness for you to be married now—at the very threshold of your artistic life. Very few great singers have married early. Lind, Patti, Kellogg, were all well into their careers before they thought of marriage."

"Melba was married," I said.

"And is divorced," Lina replied. "A singer is not an ordinary woman—she needs her freedom, she needs to study, and above all she must go where she is called—be it one end of the world or the other. Carlo, too, must have his freedom."

"He wouldn't have been free if he'd married Carola Cartieri," I said.

"Oh, you've heard about Carola." Lina nodded. "It was well for him he did not marry her, for I have been told she was utterly selfish." She gave me a mischievous look. "And so are you, my dear Leila."

"Lina!" I exclaimed in stricken tones.

"But it is good for you to be selfish," she added. "An artist must be selfish if she is to prosper. One of Carlo's problems is that he is not selfish enough. He has given up much for his father, and if—if anything happens to the Maestro, he should have his chance. He does not need to cater to another demanding person."

"But—I—I wouldn't *be* demanding if—if he . . ." I began.

"My dear, you do not know what it is not to be demanding. It is second nature to you—you wear blinders here and here." She touched either side of my face. "And you see only ahead. My advice to you, Leila, is to keep your eyes focused in that direction as long as it is possible for you to do so—because in that way you will prosper."

Her words were disquieting. "You don't think very much of me."

"Oh, my dear, I do." she answered. "I understand you, you see. When I was your age, my world revolved around me, too. And if it's any comfort to you, I was in love at least three times before I was nineteen—with my conductor, with a certain baritone, and with a nice gentleman from the audience who sent me roses whenever I sang." She laughed. "And each time, I was sure I could not live without the man in question. Oh, it was all so tragic—but fortunately, I had wonderful recuperative powers when I was eighteen, and you do, too. Wait and see. In Sacramento, you will probably fall in love with a handsome Californian, and in Stockton, there will be another, and a third in San Francisco, which is as it should be—as long as your art remains your greatest love."

Tears stung my eyes. "I shall never fall in love with anyone else!" I replied hotly.

She sighed. "That is what I said, too—every time, my dear." Leaning back in her seat, she closed her eyes wearily. "I must rest, Leila."

I turned away from her, resenting her fiercely and coming close to actually disliking her. Not only had she given me a most unflattering reading of my character, but she had utterly failed to perceive that I was truly in love—even, though I hesitated to use the adjective, "tragically" in love—but that is how I felt. At that moment, I even resented my art, since it seemed to infer a thralldom which would rob me of those experiences I now craved. "Antonia is married!" I told myself, and then I remembered her separation from her children and her constant catering to Rinaldo. Could I do that? If I had someone I loved, I could. If I had Carlo, I could—I knew I could. Oh, if he would only come in to see us! I stared out the window, not seeing the passing landscape, seeing only Carlo and Olivia at the table and how she had smiled at him and he at her. The sound of the train wheels was loud in my ears. Eventually, it lulled me to sleep.

I awakened with Carlo's voice in my ears and found him sitting across from Lina, saying anxiously ". . . when we get to Sacramento."

"No," she demurred. "I am fine. I truly am."

"Are you?" he demanded.

"Entirely, my dear, but I am concerned about you. You deserve to be scolded."

Inwardly, I gasped. What was she going to say!

"Scolded?" Carlo raised his eyebrows. "What have I done?"

"Too much, my dear boy. You are a talented conductor and you should not neglect your art. All this rushing around—worrying about bookings, costumes, the vagaries of artists. Can't the Maestro hire a competent manager? You ought to have your chance."

I gave her a sidelong glare. Why was she advising Carlo to leave the company? Because of me, that's why! I said, "But Carlo conducts every night."

"Every night on the road will not make his reputation!" Lina exclaimed. "He needs to go to a big city—New York, London, Paris, Milano."

"He will be in San Francisco," I said.

"Lina is right," Carlo said. "And after San Francisco, there is the chance that I will go to New York."

Lina's eyes glistened. "Will you?"

"Nothing is certain yet, but Father and I have discussed it. There has been an offer . . ."

Lina's eyes narrowed, "Does the Maestro object?"

"No, he thinks I should go—but I wonder if I should leave him."

A "no" trembled on my lips, but before I could speak, Lina said, "Carlo, my dear, you shouldn't think twice about it. You should go. He can get another conductor. Many would be delighted at the chance to work with the troupe. You owe to yourself to take this opportunity—be selfish for once, my dear."

He smiled at her. "Dear Lina, you are always so wise." He kissed her hand. "I'd better get back to Father." He barely looked at me. "I'll bid you both good afternoon."

I waited until the door had closed behind him before I said in a low angry voice, "You did that on purpose!"

Lina gave me a startled glance. "What did I do?"

"You—you're trying to separate us. That's why you advised him to go. I—I'll never forgive you!"

"Is that what you think, Leila?" she gasped.

"Yes, that's what I think!" I cried. "And you know it's true. Oh, how could you, when I love him so?"

"Oh, my poor Leila." She shook her head sadly. "You don't know the meaning of the word."

The coldness that had sprung up between Lina and me lasted until we reached the California border, then

A Shadow on the House

dispersed as, together, we rejoiced in the beautiful countryside with its green fields, its orchards, its tall spindly palm trees—and flowers everywhere! By the time we had arrived in Sacramento, I had begged her pardon, not because I thought myself in the wrong but in the interests of peace—after all, I was very fond of her. She accepted my apologies graciously, though I noticed she had none to give me. She probably imagined *herself* in the right!

There was the usual flurry at the station, and it was with a pang that I saw Carlo shepherding the leading members of the troupe toward some waiting carriges. More than ever, I resented my seclusion from them and, as a result, from Carlo, too. Then, as I watched, Rignoli suddenly threw down his suitcase, gesticulated wildly, and burst into a stream of impassioned Italian. As his voice grew louder, the Maestro moved quickly toward him, evidently trying to reason with him. His efforts seemed futile, for Rignoli's hat and cane followed his case, then he jumped up and down while the other Italian members of the company either laughed or commented in a variety of dialects. Carlo, I noticed, said nothing.

"I wonder what's happening?" I moved toward the melee.

"Dear"—Lina put a restraining hand on my shoulder—"don't get involved."

"But what's the matter with Rignoli?"

She laughed. "He's a tenor, and that is matter enough."

"Rogues and vagabonds," commented a woman behind me in a low amused voice. "The actors are come to town. They must be actors, those ridiculous little people. Don't you agree, George?"

Casting an indignant glance over my shoulder, I noted a tall, thin lady in a drab silk suit and a plain straw hat. Everything about her seemed drab and plain —her hair, unbecomingly arranged in a cumbersome knot at the back of her head, was a dull brown, her skin was sallow, and her features unremarkable; only her eyes were arresting. Deep-set and a bright hazel, they had a sardonic gleam that annoyed me until the man she had addressed as George said, "I do not think they are actors, Kezia. I have the feeling they are Mother's opera singers."

I moved closer to Lina. "Did you hear that?" I whispered.

She gave me a startled look. "Hear what?" she asked, far too loudly for my comfort.

"Nothing!" I said hastily, adding, "I wonder if I left my gloves in the train? I turned back toward the tracks, letting my eyes rest on a middle distance including the man who had just made that extraordinary statement.

"You're wearing your gloves, Leila," Lina said.

"Oh," I whirled back, holding up my hand and laughing affectedly, "So I am. My goodness, I am absentminded!" It was with a real effort that I kept my eyes on her when directly in back of me stood one of the most handsome men I had ever seen! His features were still imprinted on my mind, and there was something about him that had intrigued me. In addition to being good-looking, his face was tantalizingly familiar. I had seen it somewhere before, though I could not remember where. While I puzzled over it, the woman said, "We'd better be getting back. It's a pity Aunt Aurelia couldn't have been with us—she would probably have second thoughts about entertaining such a motley crew."

"I am sure Mother would not mind their behavior if she liked their music," he said.

"Leila, Lina!" Startled, I looked up to see Carlo striding toward us through the crowds. "I've been looking for you," he said abruptly. "Father has a hack waiting. We'll drive you to your hotel."

His sudden appearance effectively banished all thought of the couple behind me, especially since he held out his arm to me a split second before he made the same gesture to Lina. As I took it, I asked, "Is the argument settled?"

"Argument?" he repeated.

"Between Rignoli and you?"

"Oh, that," he shrugged. "I never argue with Rignoli —he argues with me and I do not listen."

"Bravo," Lina approved. "How did you become so wise, Carlo?"

"I do not know if you can call it wisdom—it is only a matter of conserving my energy for my performances. Rignoli thrives on altercation. I do not."

"Do you never lose your temper?" I asked wonderingly.

Unexpectedly, he tensed. "Rarely," he said sharply. "I have found it too costly an indulgence." There was a grim expression around his mouth and a hardness to his eyes. I wondered what it might signify, but before I could probe further, we were at the carriage. He was about to help Lina inside when someone near us exclaimed passionately, *"Aiuto,* signor!"

Startled, we looked around to find Mario Rampolo trembling and peering into the crowds. He was making a peculiar gesture with two of his fingers. *"Aiuto,* signor!" he cried again, rolling his eyes heavenward.

"What is he doing?" I demanded.

"He is invoking God's help to save his soul. He believes he has seen a *jettatura."* Carlo smiled derisively.

"Oh, dear." Lina laughed ruefully. "Poor Mario, he is so superstitious."

"What is a *jettatura?"* I asked.

"It is a person with the evil eye," Carlo explained.

"Oh, where?" I demanded excitedly, trying to find in which direction Mario was looking.

Carlo said, "Are you so eager to encounter evil, Leila?"

"I've never seen an evil eye!" I exclaimed.

"And you never will," Lina told me tartly, "because there's no such thing!" Placing her hand on Carlo's arm, she added, "May we not go to our hotel now? I am very tired."

"Immediately," he said, lifting her in his arms and placing her gently in the carriage.

"Carlo!" she protested, laughing.

I looked at her enviously, wishing that I, too, might have pleaded a similar lassitude; since I could not, I had to settle for the hand he held out to me. As I touched his fingers, a little tingle similar to an electric shock buzzed up my arm. His hand tightened on mine and from the sudden gleam in his eye, I had the feeling he had experienced a similar sensation. I wished we might prolong the contact, but all too quickly he dropped my hand, and though he sat directly across from me, he did not look at me. Instead, he turned to his father, saying, "I think we should not drive by the state capitol this afternoon. Lina is tired. She must go immediately to her hotel."

"Eh?" the Maestro had evidently been dozing, for he stared at Carlo blankly.

"And you are tired, too." Carlo smiled at his father, then said to the driver, "To the Hotel Mirabel, as quickly as possible, please." Facing Lina, he added, "You ought to see a doctor."

"No," she said stubbornly. "I only need rest."

"You also deserve a scolding," he said pointedly.

She put her hand on his arm. "Please, dear, I am enjoying myself. I truly am."

Carlo's eyes were troubled. "I will not argue with you . . . ."

"Don't," she begged.

"Yet . . . "

"You said you would not argue," she reminded him.

I found their conversation confusing. "Argue about what?"

"I wish you might understand, Leila," Carlo said.

"Understand what?"

"It is not important!" Lina told me.

"No?" Carlo demanded.

"No." She shook her head.

Feeling resentful and excluded, I stared out the window and found myself looking directly into the face of the man from the station! He and his companion were seated in an open carriage, and as they passed from view, I realized where I had seen him—in my textbook of English literature! Except that his skin was deeply tanned and his hair a sun-bleached gold, he looked exactly like my favorite poet—Lord Byron! I remembered, too, Mrs. Sully, our English teacher, quoting Lady Caroline Lamb's description of him: "Mad, bad and dangerous to know." Might that also apply to the man from the station? And what had he meant by "mother's opera singers"?

"Look, Leila." Carlo's hand was on my shoulder. "There's the old Cooper mansion—it's quite a landmark in this town."

"Where?" I asked.

"Over there," he pointed. "All those turrets and cupolas. See? The people who settled Sacramento ran to architectural excesses."

Though I gazed at the large ugly mansion dutifully enough, I was more interested in the fact that Carlo had not removed his hand from my shoulder. The tingly feeling had returned and Lord Byron was banished from my thoughts.

Three days later, I had sung another successful *Traviata* and I had also learned the identity of the man I had christened "Lord Byron." His full name was George Fowler and he—with his mother, the immensely wealthy Aurelia Fowler, and his cousin, Kezia Graves—lived in one of those architecturally excessive houses Carlo had mentioned. Among its numerous features was a completely equipped private theater to which our company—or "motley crew"—had been engaged to present a concert for Mrs. Fowler and her guests, among whom were the governor of the state and various members of the legislature. After the entertainment, there would be a grand bal masqué given in the famed Yellow Pavillion of that mansion, which was officially known as La Casa d'oro after the golden metal that had originally enriched the Fowler family. Unofficially, according to Mr. Hyams, the stage manager of the Sacramento Theater, Mrs. Fowler's abode was called the "Sore Thumb," for reasons which would be obvious to us when we saw it, he groaned—adding that in his opinion it was incredibly ugly!

Naturally, given the snatch of conversation I had overheard at the station, I was intensely eager to see it—in fact, in the four intervening days before the event, I could think of little else in those few moments when I had leisure to think. In addition to preparing our program for the concert, we were also rehearsing the "Cav" and "Pag" to be presented the Tuesday following the Sunday we were to perform at the Fowler estate.

When I was not rehearsing or being coached, Lina and I walked through the city, which, in spite of its flowers and trees, was something of a disappointment to us since it lacked the Spanish flavor we had expected to find throughout California. Sacramento had been settled by the miners and by Yankee storekeepers who had come there in the wake of the gold rush—and also, though its citizens did not boast of the fact, by Australian convicts. Consequently, people of Irish, English, and German origin were in far more abundance than those of Mexican or Spanish descent, and the wide streets of the town were flanked by big wooden or brick mansions, while the business district, Lina said, resembled that of any mid-Western town. Still, the climate was lovely; there was a dearth of rain, and the air was scented by orange blossoms. It was the sort of weather that made me feel lazy and at the same time full of vague cravings. Several times Carlo had chided me for being inattentive at rehearsal. "You look at me," he had said on one occasion, "but you do not hear! Where are you?"

I had been unable to answer him, unable to defend myself; I had no defense. It was terrible to see so much of him yet be separated from him by the wall of his indifference, immersed in his work, he seemed oblivious of everyone—even Olivia Seton, who, I noticed, appeared very discontented, flouncing about the stage and glaring at him whenever he spoke to her. I noticed, too, that she no longer waited for him after rehearsals; but that, in itself, was small comfort since he did not seek my company either, but went his way alone. Thus I really craved the diversion offered by our day in the country, and finally it arrived!

I dressed with particular care that morning. I wore a dainty white shirtwaist with a lace collar fastened at the throat with a green jade brooch Mama had given me. My skirt and cloak were also green and there was a single curling green feather on my straw hat; I had packed my golden silk gown for the concert, and all in all, I was reasonably sure that George Fowler's sharp-tongued cousin Kezia would not be able to term me part of a "motley crew."

I finished my toilet early, but I need not have hurried since Lina did not rise until after ten. She took a long time to dress, far too long to my way of thinking, but when I mildly suggested that we might be late, she grew quite cross and said sharply that I might go by myself if I choose—which of course I would not do, as well she knew. It was close to noon when we finally climbed into the hired hack that was to take us out to the estate. We would be, I thought disconsolately, the very last ones to arrive, and I would be deprived of more than an hour of that eagerly anticipated outing.

I was very cool to Lina on our way to the country, but if she was aware of my displeasure, she said nothing. Despite the fact that she had slept so late that morning, she dozed during much of the ride, waking only when we were nearing the Casa d'oro. We both gaped in amazement at one of the most incredible piles of masonry either one of us had ever seen!

Though it was set well back from the road and surrounded by trees, it had been built on a rise, and thus its roof and at least half a story were easily evident. Constructed of stone, bricks, and, apparently, gold, its main part was designed along gothic lines, ending in a tall churchlike steeple, flanked on one side by a tesselated Norman tower and on the other by the golden dome of what appeared to be an Eastern mosque.

Our carriage came to a sudden halt as the driver,

who had been far from loquacious thus far, turned back to comment, "Some showplace, ain't it?"

There was no arguing with him. "It—it looks like something out of a nigh— dream," I said.

"Yep," the driver nodded. "It's some showplace."

"How old is it?" Lina asked.

"Um—maybe forty—nope, more like fifty-odd years old. Built 'round 1851 or 1852 . . . disremember which year it went up. . . . Old Fowler it was that done it . . ." He sent a stream of tobacco-tinged spittle into the bushes—it may or may not have been a comment. "Had hisself a mine," he continued. "Made a mint. That there house cost him over seventy-five thousand dollars. Young Mrs. Fowler, her that has it now, brung the furniture from all over . . . fixtures in the bathrooms made of pure gold. Got a passel of English servants—nobody 'round here'd work the place even if they was asked."

"Why not?" I demanded.

"Got a bad name," the driver said. "Yep, got a bad name."

"What does that mean?" I questioned.

He shrugged. "People livin' there ain't lucky. Old Fowler's two kids, they wasn't lucky an' neither's his grandson . . . . Nope, there's none of 'em lucky."

"Why aren't . . . "

Lina tapped me on the shoulder. "Let's get on our way," she said impatiently. "It's very dusty on these roads." She looked up at the driver. "Is it much further?"

"No, ma'am, not much." He flicked his whip.

As we moved forward, I said, "I wish you'd let me ask him what he meant."

"Oh, I can't bear this talk of luck," she snapped. "It's only superstition. There's no such thing as luck. If the inhabitants of that monstrosity haven't been lucky, I'm sure it's their fault. I wouldn't feel lucky living in that, myself."

"They must be very rich, though," I said. "Seventy-five thousand dollars and gold faucets, fancy!"

"That money should've been put to better use," Lina said dryly.

A few minutes later, we reached a pair of iron gates, which were shut and barred. We had to wait until a burly man emerged from a narrow house that looked, Lina said, like a larger version of a sentry's box. He had a paper with him.

"Name?" he rasped.

"Miss Paulina Da Costa and Miss Leila MacKenzie," I said importantly.

He glanced at his list. "Not here."

"Not there . . . " I began indignantly.

"Shhhh," Lina leaned forward. "We are with the Benedetto Opera Troupe."

He glanced at the list a second time. "All right, I'll let you in." Ambling back to the gates, he opened them and we drove through.

"That man!" I fumed.

"He was only doing his job."

"We should have been on the list!"

"Why? We're not guests—we're entertainers. At least you are."

"Melba would have been on the list!" I cried.

"You're being foolish, Leila."

"I . . . " I subsided. It was useless to argue. I knew I was being foolish, but still I could not help feeling humiliated at being one of a group, when I was so very much myself. Some day, I vowed, I should be so famous and so rich that no one would need to consult a list when I entered a gate—they would know me on sight and they would fall at my feet and kiss the hem of my gown!

"Look at the gardens!" Lina exclaimed.

Glancing toward them, I gasped in amazement at vast beds of roses, daisies, pansies, and numerous other blossoms for which I had no names. There were also flowering trees and bushes and, among these, a plethora of statuary ranging from stone dwarfs to pitcher-bearing maidens. I counted three fishponds and two fountains. It was Lina who first pointed out the stone summerhouse reflected in yet another pool. Then, rounding a bend in the road, our attention was once more captured by the Casa d'oro. Its facade conformed to its roof—the Norman part was square and massive with small slitlike windows; the Gothic portion ran to arched windows and a truly massive front door set in a carved stone alcove topped by a bas-relief representing three gaunt medieval angels; the dome swelled into a round tower fashioned from vari-colored bricks forming a zigzag design. Its windows were covered with a stone lattice that Lina described as "Moorish."

"The Sore Thumb," I said, and giggled.

"The what?" Lina demanded.

I told her about Mr. Hyams's description and she burst into laughter. "It certainly is!"

"I can hardly wait to see what it's like inside!" I exclaimed.

"It looks," Lina mused, "as if it could swallow us whole."

"Brrrr." I shivered. "What a thing to say!" Yet as we started toward the door, I found myself in agreement with her. It seemed to me that the house was vaguely sinister, as if the coupling—or rather the tripling—of styles had been happy neither in execution or in effect.

We were not destined to see much of the interior. Our ring was answered by a black-clad butler whose accent and bearing proclaimed him one of the English servants mentioned by the driver. We were ushered into a lofty hall with an open-timbered roof, heavily carved and centered by a hanging glass globe in which the gas fixtures had been replaced by electricity. The floor was tiled, and in the middle was a fountain in which a bronze fish spurted streams of water into a marble basin. Beyond the fountain was an archway, through which we saw a stained-glass window patterned with lilies and violets. There were several doors, all closed.

Indicating two ornately carved wooden chairs standing on either side of an inlaid marble table, the butler said, "You will please to wait here. I shall announce you to Madame."

"Well?" Lina inquired as soon as we were alone, "does it live up to your expectations?"

"It's very grand," I whispered.

"And very ugly—as well as cold. It reminds me of the inside of a cathedral—or a sepulcher."

I could have wished she had not made that particular comparison, for I had been thinking that despite its richness, it was even more daunting and depressing inside than out. "It does seem to have a lugubrious air, and I can't say I like those ugly faces carved on the doors!"

"Dragons and gargoyles." Lina laughed. "And speaking of gargoyles, I wonder if that is a portrait of Mr. Fowler?"

"Where?"

"Back of you."

I looked up and gasped as I saw the likeness of a gaunt old man with heavy brows and piercing brown eyes that seemingly glared into mine. His nose was straight and thin; his mouth, also thin, curved downward grimly, and there were deep furrows on either side of it. He had been depicted standing with one hand on a desk; the arm that hung at his side ended in a clenched fist.

"His eyes . . . " I whispered. "I've seen eyes like that before."

Lina grimaced. "He looks as though he would like to step out of that frame and strike someone."

"Very well put," a voice behind us observed. "My grandfather struck often and cruelly."

Lina and I whirled to face the tall woman I had first seen in the railroad station. On meeting her eyes, I knew why those of the portrait had seemed so familiar. "Miss Graves," I said.

She frowned, and her resemblance to her grandfather became even more marked. "Have we met?" she inquired. "I do not think I . . . "

I could feel the flush on my cheeks. "No, no, we haven't met," I said hurriedly. "It—it's only that I knew you lived here . . . "

"I see . . . " Her voice slashed through my explanations like a knife. "You were quite right—I am Miss Graves. Bartram tells me that you are with the singers?"

Again I had lost my individuality and again I did not like it. "I am Miss MacKenzie," I told her, "and this is Miss Da Costa, and yes, we are with the singers."

Barely acknowledging my introduction, she said coldly, "You will want to join your friends, no doubt." Opening the front door, she waved us through. "I will take you to them."

We followed her to a gravel pathway that extended around the eastern tower, then angled off across another expanse of garden to a building resembling a small church, complete with tower and rose window. However, when Miss Graves opened its door, we saw an auditorium, equipped with some two hundred seats, a balcony, boxes, and a sizable stage—indeed, it was deeper and wider than the one on which I had made my debut.

"My grandfather built this to harbor wandering evangelists," Miss Graves said, "but my aunt redesigned the interior. Your company is outside. We are serving lunch in the Shakespearean gardens. Come."

Planted with the flowers and trees mentioned in the poet's plays, the garden was located directly in back of the theater and behind a high hedge of cedars. "You'll find it very pleasant," Miss Graves said as she neared a wooden gate. "It is completely sequestered. You and your friends will be safe from the prying eyes of curious intruders."

Her words were gracious, but the lightly satirical tone in which they were uttered hinted that the real purpose of this privacy was to keep the "motley crew" from mingling with her aunt's distinguished visitors. It was at that moment that I began to hate her. No, hate is too strong a term, but certainly I disliked her.

Yet, when a girl from the chorus, shortly after she

had left us, aped her way of walking and talking, I was humiliated rather than amused by antics Miss Graves would have termed ill-bred. More than ever I was aware that the cedars were barriers to keep us out, and this realization robbed me of much of my enjoyment. I felt socially degraded, and even though there was a lovely repast served to us in that truly beautiful garden, I longed to join those guests who would be welcomed in the salons of that great house.

The other members of the Benedetto Troupe did not appear to notice they were being ostracized. As lighthearted as children, they wandered up and down the garden paths, playing tag and generally enjoying themselves; for once I did not resent my isolation from them. I was quite content to sit next to Lina on a rustic bench in the corner of the garden known as "the forest of Arden" by virtue of two large English oak trees.

Lina did not have much to say. For the most part, she leaned back against her seat with her eyes closed. I was glad of her silence, for I was busy with my own thoughts—which for once did not revolve around Carlo. I was remembering the man I had seen at the station and wondering if he would come into our garden. Probably not, but perhaps I would see him at the ball, unless they found another special room for us to dance in. I was sure that if Miss Graves had her way, we would be locked away from our "betters."

In the midst of these bitter ruminations, an acorn dropped into my lap, followed by two more. I glanced up, startled, and was even more startled to look full into Carlo's laughing eyes. "Oh!" I leaped to my feet. "What are you doing in that tree?"

He had balanced himself against a forked branch. "I had the fancy to climb a tree," he said. "It is a long time since I have seen such a fine one."

"Carlo!" Lina had opened her eyes. "Be careful, you'll fall!"

"I have never fallen from a tree," he told her with a mischievous grin, which made him look very boyish, especially since his hair was tousled and his shirt open at the throat. "Would you like to join me, Leila?" he actually winked at me.

"No!" Lina protested. "Don't be ridiculous, she could hurt herself!"

I gave her an annoyed glance. "It looks easy enough, I would just have to ease myself up on that limb and . . . " I circled the tree.

"Leila, I absolutely forbid your doing anything of the kind!" Lina cried.

"But . . . "

"No, you must not argue with your wise guardian," Carlo counseled. "Lina always knows what is best. I will come down." Climbing out of the tree quickly, he came over to us. "Would you object to a stroll around the gardens? You may accompany us, Lina, to be sure I do not make her climb a tree."

"No," Lina said, much to my relief. "You have my permission to stroll. I prefer to sit here. It's a comfortable corner."

Carlo moved to my side. *"Dammi il braccio, mia piccina,"* he murmured.

"Oh," I said, laughing. "I know that."

"You do?" He raised his eyebrows.

I nodded, singing softly, *"Obbedisco, signor."*

"Brava!" He clapped his hands. "You do know it, Mademoiselle Mimi. Are you familiar with all of *La Bohème?*"

"All of Mimi," I answered. "It was my first role. I'd love to sing it sometime."

"Perhaps you will," he said.

"Oh, Carlo, when?"

He smiled at me. "Come, I refuse to talk business this afternoon. Let us look at this lovely place."

It was particularly lovely viewed from Carlo's side when he was so pleasant, too. Much to my delight, he deliberately avoided the rest of the company, much of which was still congregated near the tables. We took a path that ran along a small stream that gushed over a series of rocks down to a pond bordered by willow trees. Near it was a small marble bench.

"Come, Leila," Carlo said. "Let's see if there are any goldfish in the pool." Grasping my hand, he led me down a grassy slope. A minute later we were seated on the bench peering into the silvery water.

"I don't see any goldfish," I began. "I . . ." I froze. "Carlo . . ." I breathed. "What . . . what's that white thing—down there? It . . . it looks like an arm."

"An arm . . . ?" he repeated incredulously.

"Look," I pointed. "There at the edge."

He rose and went to the edge of the pool, then he laughed, albeit rather shakily. "But it is an arm," he said. "And it is attached to a body. Come and look, Leila."

"A body? A dead body?" I quavered.

"Not a dead body. To be a dead body it would have needed to have been alive, and unless there is a Pygmalion in our midst, this never lived."

Joining him, I looked down into the water at the beautifully sculpted statue of a drowned girl. Snaky marble vines were twisted through her long marble locks, and one arm still clung to the bank. She was covered with a faint green growth of moss. "Oh," I shuddered. "Ophelia!"

"Yes," he said. "Ophelia."

Still shuddering, I turned away, "I don't like it." Tears started to my eyes. "Oh, Carlo, I just don't like it," I repeated.

His arms were around me. "No, it is not pleasant," he agreed. "The mind that would plan such a thing is not a nice mind, but you mustn't cry, little Leila. It is only a statue."

"I—I am sorry," I murmured, clinging to him.

"You must not be sorry, either." He was holding me tightly, and suddenly he kissed me hard. I felt his heart beating against my breast, but almost immediately, he drew back from me. "I—I am sorry," he said quickly.

"You must not be sorry, either," I smiled at him mistily, hoping he would remember his own words.

"I—should not have done that," he said in a choked voice. "It was not right—you are only a little girl . . . "

"I am not a little girl!" I cried indignantly. "I am eighteen!"

A slight smile hovered about his mouth. "Ah, yes, eighteen—an ancient spinster lady. But . . . " He frowned. "You must not think . . . I mean . . . " He broke off. "I wish you would not look at me in such a way!"

"In what sort of a way?" I asked, moving closer to him and putting my hands on his shoulders, clasping them lightly around his neck. "Tell me," I whispered, wanting no words from him, wanting only his lips on mine again.

He bent toward me, then stepped back. "No. no, no." Gently he removed my clinging hands. "It must not happen. I will not let it happen." He glared at me. "One of us must be wise. I will take you back to Lina."

"I do not need you to take me back!" I cried angrily. "I will go alone." I fled from him then, running up the slope, but I did not return to Lina immediately—instead, I walked in another part of the garden. I was inclined to cry, yet I was also ecstatically happy because Carlo had kissed me, and as Mama had always said, "Actions speak louder than words." All in all, I would not cry, I decided, because sooner or later, he would also say the words I wanted to hear. I was positive, well—almost positive—of that.

During the latter part of the afternoon, we rehearsed. The acoustics of the hall were excellent; even Olivia Seton, whose vocal technique left much to be desired, sounded well. The musicians liked the pit, especially since each music stand had been electrically wired. The stage lighting, too, was fine—again, it was better than that of the theater in which I had made my debut. One of the English servants from the house served as technician, and from him we learned that the theater was rarely used. It seemed a shame.

After rehersal, there was a supper served in the so-called green room of the theater; this was in the basement near the dressing rooms, which were also well-equipped. I saw very little of Carlo but that was to be expected, since he was busy with a variety of tasks and since, given the circumstances in which we had parted, he would naturally avoid me. I rested for the hour before it was time to dress, and I had a dream—not of Carlo. I was back in the garden looking at that sunken statue, and it seemed to me that the marble was flesh-colored and that the drowned girl was trying to rise from the water, struggling and weeping, the while her nether limbs were slowly turning to marble again. It was a strange dream—I was glad to awaken from it.

Precisely at 7:30, the theater was opened by several servants in livery, with powdered wigs and silk stockings—looking, as Antonia remarked, like members of a court band. The curtain, a golden damask, had no peephole through which to scan the audience, but it was possible to peer through the side; and though Lina maintained that "counting the house" was sadly amateurish, I did it a few minutes before we began. The impression I received was not entirely felicitous. Many of the people were of a type I knew well from Denver —hard-bitten, craggy-looking men, uncomfortable in stiff shirts and formal attire, heavy-set women with grim mouths and small cold eyes, some of them so sunburned that the division between red neck and white chest was ludicrous. Also ludicrous were some of the costumes—elaborate eighteenth century or renaissance dress does not go well with muscular arms, calloused hands, and sagging bosoms. I drew back, thinking that the "motley crew" was not necessarily on my side of the curtain. It also occurred to me that I had not seen "Lord Byron"; perhaps he did not share his mother's enthusiasm for music.

At eight, Carlo struck up the overture from *Zampa* and we began. It went very well. The audience was attentive and, much to my surprise, singularly appreciative. After I had sung "Ah fors' è lui" and "Sempre Libera" as well as Marguerite's Jewel Song from *Faust*,

I was cheered as well as applauded—and so were most of the other singers. There was only one jarring note to the evening and that was provided by Mario Rampolo, who, in the midst of singing Valentin's "Farewell," also from *Faust,* suddenly froze into complete silence and, according to Clara Petrucci, who was watching from the wings, made that peculiar gesture with his two fingers. He recovered himself an instant later, finished to polite if not enthusiastic applause, and rushed backstage. Lina and I saw him weeping and shaking in the corridor near the stage door.

"*Strega . . . strega . . .* " he was muttering.

"Oh, Mario, there are no witches!" Lina soothed.

He did not appear to have heard her. Crossing himself more than once, he babbled, "I must go. I will not stay where there is such evil. No, I will not stay!" Wrenching open the door, he dashed out and did not return.

Fortunately, Emilio Jacopo could cover for him, and he was not missed. After the concert, we congregated in the green room to receive the plaudits of Mrs. Fowler's guests. The first person to appear was Mrs. Fowler herself. She came in followed by her son, who was, I noted, more handsome than ever in his beautifully tailored evening clothes. However, it was his mother who caught one's eye—a little above medium height, she was a husky woman with strong features, wide gray eyes, and luxuriant brown-gray hair which she had piled untidily on top of her head and fastened with a diamond clip. Her gown was scarlet silk, glittering with sequins and bugle beads and a truly magnificent diamond necklace. More diamonds glistened on her fingers, from the several bracelets she wore on each arm, from her ears, and even from the buckles on her shoes. Yet despite all this ostentatious display, she gave the impression of being forthright, down-to-earth, and even kindly. Unlike Miss Graves, she spoke with a pronounced Western twang, saying loudly, "I want to speak to the little chicken who sang the *Traviata*—I like her."

Her son glanced quickly around the room, and much to my secret delight, he saw me immediately and smiled. "I believe this is the young lady, Mother," he said, coming directly to me. "You sang delightfully, Miss MacKenzie," he said.

"Thank you," I replied, pleased that he had remembered my name from the program.

His mother looked at me sharply. "Yep, nothin' but a chicken," she repeated, "but you don't squawk like one. How old are you anyhow?"

"I am eighteen, Mrs. Fowler," I said.

"Eighteen!" she boomed. She looked up at her son, "Eighteen." She shook her head. "It sure beats all. I didn't think any of them divas was under thirty." She clasped my hand warmly—painfully, too, since her rings pressed into my flesh.

I managed a gratified smile. "I am glad I pleased you."

"You sure did, honey, you sure did. I liked your singin' and I liked your spunk. Ain't many girls eighteen years old'd stand up there cool as a cucumber and emote in Eyetalian—not even the Eyetalians can always do it. What happened to that feller came apart at the seams in the middle of his song?"

Tactfully, I answered, "I—believe he was ill."

"Ill? Looked scared silly to me!"

"I don't know," I said.

"Well, nobody missed him." She grasped my hand again. "I do admire spunk," she repeated, then, much to my relief, she released my hand and went on to speak to the rest of the soloists.

As she moved away, Miss Graves took her place. As usual, she was unbecomingly dressed—this time in a high-necked gown of violet silk that could not have been a worse choice considering her coloring. She said coldly, "You seem to have pleased my aunt."

"I am glad if I have," I answered.

"You did very well," she commented. "It is a voice of promise, Miss—uh—MacKinny?"

"MacKenzie," I corrected, smiling at her sweetly and longing to hit her.

"Oh, yes, I am so bad on names I do not hear very often," she replied. "I do hope you will continue to pursue this—calling. You should have quite a success when you are older."

"You are very encouraging," I said, aware now that she was deliberately trying to insult me. I wondered why, but before I had time to speculate further on the matter, Mrs. Fowler's booming voice filled the room.

"You are all invited to the Yellow Pavillion, now—and if any of you don't have masks, there's a whole heap of 'em near the door as you go in."

And so, at last, Cinderella was about to enter the enchanted domain of the rich—nor was my enthusiasm for the venture dulled by my glimpse of its denizens. The exhilaration of singing was still upon me, and I needed the excitement that the ball would bring. Perhaps, despite his earlier attitude, Carlo would be my Prince Charming, even if only for a few magic hours. Consequently, it was with a light heart and a light step that I hurried across the darkened gardens in the wake of the servants who were leading us to the Yellow Pavillion. I would have walked faster, but Lina had said in a spent voice that she could not rush. I was a little annoyed with her—as I have said, from early morning on, she had seemed determined to spoil my pleasure that day. I could not get her to talk or to do much of anything except seek the nearest available chair and sit down. She had hardly commented about my performance—indeed, she seemed almost angry with me, though I could not think why. Just before we arrived at the ballroom, I asked her if anything was troubling her.

She looked at me a long moment before she answered, "What do you think might be troubling me, Leila?"

"I don't know," I exclaimed. "That's why I asked. I hope it's nothing I've done."

She laughed. "But Leila, my dear, you've done nothing!"

"Well, that's a relief," I said; then, as her laughter continued, I inquired, "Have I said something funny?"

Shaking her head, she continued to laugh. I decided she must have drunk too much champagne that afternoon. Then I forgot all about her peculiar mood, for we had arrived at the round tower, and through the open door I heard the music of a waltz. Much as the bemused children of Hamelin followed their piper, I followed it through that portal. Someone handed me a mask. I slipped it on and stepped through an archway into the most magnificent chamber in the world—at least so I thought at the time.

Actually, I have not changed my opinion. I do not believe I have seen anything to surpass the Yellow Pavillion. The first impression I had was of light, light reflected from the bright polished circular floor which occupied the entire circumference of the tower. More light blazed at me from the curved mirrors that covered the walls. As I grew accustomed to the glitter, I saw that most of it came from the huge crystal chandelier that descended from the lofty dome; it had been electrified and in place of its many candles were small incandescent bulbs. Above the mirrors and around the entire dome ran a small wooden balcony, its railing carved and gilded oak. It was reached by a flight of stairs near the door; chairs were arranged on the balcony, and there sat those women who did not want to dance; across from them on the other side of the building were musicians. The dome was fancifully painted with cabalistic signs—black on gold. It was a room out of a fairy tale—truly, it was an enchanted place, for the people I had seen when I peeped through the curtain had vanished, and in that vast golden globe of a room, the masked creatures who whirled in time to the music seemed to have come from another world.

As I watched in a veritable trance of delight, someone asked me to dance. Without even looking at him, I drifted into his arms. His grasp was firm, he moved with consummate grace, but as we circled that immense floor, I was hardly aware of him. The music had claimed me, and only when it ended, did I look up at my partner. Though he was masked, I recognized him by his height, by his sun-bleached hair, and by the shape of his face—he was "Lord Byron."

"Oh!" I breathed.

He smiled down at me, his blue eyes glinting through the slits of his mask. "A waltz to remember!" he said.

"Oh, yes, only . . ."

"Only it ended far too soon," he finished for me. Was that what I had meant to say? I was not sure, but it was the truth. "There will be another," he told me. "May I have it?"

Before I could answer him, the strains of the promised waltz echoed through the room. I was in his arms again, and as he swept me away, I caught sight of a mirror, which, in the reflecting glass across from us, multiplied us into a thousand, thousand couples dancing down an endless corridor. I had the absurd and frightening fancy that we had sold our souls to the music and were condemned to dance forever on that golden path to nowhere. Then, a hand was on my shoulder and Carlo said urgently, "Thank God I've found you, Leila. You must come with me."

I stopped mid-step. "With you?" I repeated stupidly.

"Look here, old man," my partner began, "can't you wait until . . ."

"No," Carlo cut him off sharply. "Lina is ill—she's had a seizure . . ."

I clutched his arm. "Lina—ill? Where is she? What's happened?"

"This way," Carlo took my arm. "They've taken her out . . ."

"They . . . who . . . what's wrong . . . ? She's . . . she's not . . ."

"No," he said quickly. "Fortunately, there's a doctor

among the guests. He's with her now, but I'm afraid she's quite ill."

They had brought her to the library, connected to the ballroom by a long corridor. Near the end of it, we found Antonia, Rinalda, and the Maestro, huddled on a couch and looking disturbed. Antonia was crying softly. "Oh, Leila," she sobbed as I passed her, "she looks so—white!"

I barely heeded her. I rushed into an immense book-lined chamber, looking wildly around me. "Where is she?" I cried frantically.

"Over here," Carlo led me to a long leather sofa, where Mrs. Fowler and a small, bald-headed man were standing. "Is she any better?" he asked.

Mrs. Fowler shook her head. "It's a bad attack."

Even before I reached the sofa, I heard the terrible wheezing and agonized gasping for air. "Lina, what's the matter?" I knelt beside her. She was terribly pale, and one small hand was pressed against her heaving chest. Her eyes were closed. "What is it?" I asked.

"Asthma," the bald-headed man said. "Whatever made her come out here today, over these dusty roads? She must have known it was coming on—she should've rested!"

"How could she know?" I cried.

"It's not her first seizure," he answered. "From her condition, I'd say she'd suffered from the malady a long time."

"She has, but she was better—she was much, much better. She was practically recovered."

"You don't recover from asthma," Mrs. Fowler told me. "It stays with you." She touched my shoulder. "Come away from her, my dear. Let Dr. Adams attend to her."

I sank down on a chair. "It—it's my fault." I wept. "I should've known she wasn't feeling well, but—but . . ." I could not go on; I buried my face in my hands.

Carlo bent over me. "Do not cry," he said gently. "You could not have known . . . " He paused as the sound of her labored breathing reached us. "What are we to do?" he muttered distractedly. "How can she be helped, Doctor?"

"She must have complete rest," he answered.

"A hospital?" Carlo demanded.

Dr. Adams pulled at his lip. "Ummm, I don't recommend that she be moved at present. It would be highly dangerous to send her back over those roads in her condition."

"But . . . " Carlo began.

"She don't need to be moved," Mrs. Fowler stated decisively. "She'll stay right here."

"Yes, of course, she must stay here," a voice behind us agreed.

Startled, I looked up to find my erstwhile partner standing just inside the door. Mrs. Fowler glanced at him. "I'm glad you agree, George. Now—we can't all be in here, so you'd best go back to our guests, and where's Kezia?"

"I don't know," he answered. "Shall I look for her?"

"No," Mrs. Fowler replied. "You do as I said. Kezia's not needed here."

"Very well, Mother." He gave me a passing smile. "Now don't worry, Miss MacKenzie, she's in very good hands. Dr. Adams is the best physician in three counties!"

Carlo looked after him gratefully. "You are both so kind," he said to Mrs. Fowler.

"Kind!" she snorted. "It's the least we can do. God knows we've plenty of room—there's only the three of us jostling about in this barracks." She looked at Paulina. "She ought to be put to bed this instant. I'll have a room made up."

Moaning, Lina clutched the doctor's arm. "Please," she mouthed.

"Yes?" He bent down quickly, listening carefully as she spoke in labored whispers. "I see . . . " He soothed her. "Yes, I understand . . . . Now please don't try to talk anymore. You must not tax yourself more than is necessary. . . . " He faced me. "She says she cannot leave the young lady."

"Oh, Lina," I sobbed. "I will be all right. Truly I will."

With an almost imperceptible shake of her head, she mouthed, "No . . ."

"The young lady?" Mrs. Fowler asked, cocking an eye at me. "Her?"

"She has been traveling with her as her chaperon," Carlo explained.

"I see." Mrs. Fowler smiled. "Very fitting and proper—girl her age needs looking after. Well, they can both stay, until Miss Lina here is fit to be moved. How soon would you say that'd be, Dr. Adams?"

He shrugged. "I wouldn't want to make any predictions, Mrs. Fowler. She's a very sick woman."

"No matter," she said. "However long it takes, she can stay"—she glanced at me—"and you with her." Crossing to the window, she pulled a cord beside it. "I'll have a couple rooms made up."

"But—I can't stay out here . . . I am to sing . . . I . . ."

"Leila!" Carlo barked. "Come with me—I want to talk with you."

Dazedly, I followed him from the room and into the corridor.

"How is she?" chorused Antonia and the Maestro.

Carlo answered. I could not. Did he mean to leave me behind? But he couldn't! I was scheduled to sing on Tuesday and the following Friday and in Stockton and in San Francisco. Surely, he could not expect me to remain with Lina? Who knows how long she would be ill?

Carlo led me to a couch at the far end of the corridor. "Sit down!" he ordered. As I obeyed, he glared at me. "You shock me!" he said. "How could you think of putting an additional burden of worry on Lina at a time like this?"

"But . . ." I began.

"How could you desert her after all she has done for you?" He pounded his fist against his hand. "Have you no sense of gratitude whatsoever? I told her she should not sacrifice herself for you. I told her you did not appreciate it, and it seems I was right. I am sorry I was right. I would have preferred to be mistaken in my estimate of your character, but I see I was not. I rarely am!"

I stared at him blankly. "I—I don't understand you!" I cried.

"You don't understand, yes, I can see you don't. You have never understood just what Lina has done for you. Do you think it was easy for her to come with you when she was so ill?"

"But she said she was better . . . " I began.

"What she said and what she was—were two different things! God, have you no eyes in your head? Could you not have seen that she was ill, that it was only her iron determination that kept her going? But you did not think of that, did you? You thought only of yourself, and now you are perfectly willing to leave her here among strangers to die!"

"To d-die!" I exclaimed. "But—but the doctor didn't say . . . "

"He said she is a very sick woman. That could mean anything. God knows what it could mean if you give her more reason to worry about you. You must stay with her."

"But—but my singing. What will you do? My Nedda, my Violetta . . . Couldn't I come into town and perform them, and come back out here and maybe . . . "

"No, no, no!" He was shouting. "Is there no end to your selfishness? These people are willing to take you in, but they are not a hack service to take Madame back and forth to her engagements. Besides, I don't want you around me—your place is with Lina until she is better. We will change the bill. We have done it often enough before."

"But it's not fair. I—I can't live without singing!" I wept.

"Lina has lived without it, and she was three times the artist you are, because she had something you lack —sympathy and understanding. If the case had been reversed, do you suppose she would have put her singing ahead of you?"

My mind was in a turmoil. I was to stop singing. I was not to see Carlo any more. At this new thought, I wept afresh. "Oh, Carlo," I sobbed. "You can't leave me all by myself out here—I love you—please take me with you, please! Lina will be in good hands and I—I can come back and see her but I—singing is my life and you and—oh, dear, what's going to happen to me? I might as well be dead!"

He seized me by the shoulders, shaking me hard. "Stop it, stop it this minute! You're acting like a child. I wouldn't have you with us. No wonder Lina was so determined to shelter you from the rest of us—you are not fit to be in the company of adults! You're nothing but a spoiled, silly little girl. I wonder that Lina was willing to concern herself over you at all—you are not worth it!" Turning on his heel, he stalked down the corridor and back into the library.

I wanted to run after him and tell him I had not meant any of those things I had said, had not meant that I did not want to stay with Lina—but I knew he would not believe me. I knew, too, that he must hate me, and at that moment, something deep inside my consciousness told me that I deserved no more.

As I tried to regain my self-control, Dr. Adams, Mrs. Fowler, and Carlo came out of the library. With them was one of the liveried servants—an immense man, who was carrying Lina in his arms. At the sight of her limp figure, I forgot my own woes and sped down the hall.

"Ah," Mrs. Fowler said, "I was wonderin' where you were. Come along. We're puttin' Miss Da Costa in the Rose Suite, and we'll set up a bed for you in the sittin' room. I think you'll be comfortable enough."

"It doesn't matter," I said distractedly. "I just want to be near her." I was not speaking for effect—I meant it—but Carlo gave me a look of such icy contempt that tears ran down my cheeks again.

"Don't cry, girlie," Mrs. Fowler said soothingly. "It'll

be all right once she gets a good rest. Tomorrow we'll see about bringing Mrs. Parks in—she's good with sick people."

"You are so good," Carlo said gratefully.

"Nonsense." She smiled at him. "It's what anybody would do."

I was not looking at Carlo, but I could feel his accusing stare on me and I knew he was thinking, Anybody but Leila MacKenzie. I wanted to run from them, but I did not. I followed them into another corridor.

"We'll use the elevator, John," Mrs. Fowler said as we passed a small door. Then she moved back, startled, as it opened. Kezia Graves emerged, and Mrs. Fowler exclaimed, "There you are! Where've you been?"

Miss Graves raised her eyebrows. "I was resting in my room and Mary came to tell me what had happened." Her eyes flickered over Lina. "A shocking occurence. Of course she must be taken to a hospital at once, Aunt Aurelia!"

"Nothing of the kind, Kezia," the older woman snapped. "Dr. Adams don't advise moving her—so she and her young friend here are staying with us until such time as he thinks she's better." She looked at John. "Get in," she ordered. "You get in too, girlie. Mr. Benedetto and I will use the stairs."

In following John into the elevator, I happened to look into Miss Graves's face. I grew cold; her eyes were bright with anger—more than anger, hatred. I raised my hand, then thrust it hastily behind my back. Instinctively I made the gesture Mario Rampolo had used to ward off the evil eye!

However, when I went into the chamber where they had installed Lina, I soon forgot my momentary fears of Kezia Graves, for Lina's condition had grown even worse. There was a time in the wee hours of the morning when we all feared she might suffocate, but at last her breathing became easier. It was only after she had fallen into an exhausted slumber that Carlo left— the others had gone hours before. I saw him leave but said nothing, for during our long vigil on either side of her bed, he had not looked at me once, nor did he when he walked from her room.

Soon after Lina had fallen asleep, Dr. Adams made me go to the bed that had been set up for me in the adjoining sitting room. When I finally slipped between the covers, the sky was paling and a band of pink had appeared over the distant mountains. I did not think I would sleep, but I did.

I awakened to bright sunlight and looked about me in wonder. I had been so distraught the previous evening that I had not even noticed my surroundings; now I found myself in an exquisitely appointed chamber. Everywhere I looked, there was beauty—in the carved chairs, painted gold and covered with needlepoint embroidery depicting fantastic roses, in the commodes with their inlaid woods and golden decorations, in the gold-framed mirrors, the crystal chandelier, the ceiling with its paintings of nymphs and shepherds sporting in a rose-hued glade. The mantlepiece was of carved marble, and on it was a delicate glass and gold French clock set between two golden candelabras. The rose-colored carpet might have come from a palace, and even my small bed was lovely—its headboard had been carved in the shape of a swan's head and great carved wings fanned out on either side of me. Needless to say, I had never seen such luxury. It brought me a memory of my ambitions concerning the moguls and princes I had planned to meet and possibly marry once I became a great diva. Then, suddenly, these frivolous thoughts were swept away by the more immediate recollections of the past few hours. Jumping out of bed, I ran to the adjoining door, opening it cautiously. It swung silently back on well-oiled hinges. I passed through a small hall containing a boudoir and bath, into a chamber even more magnificent than mine. Oddly enough, I had not noticed its painted walls nor even the rose silk hangings that fell from the crowned canopy of the bed where Lina lay. Terror thrilled through me as I looked at her—her face was almost as white as the snowy pillows under her head, and to my horror, she seemed to have stopped breathing.

As I edged nearer the bed, someone said, "Let her sleep, honey. She's plumb tuckered out, poor little thing."

"Oh!" Startled, I turned to find a short plump woman in a dark blue uniform covered by a starched white apron. She had been sitting in a chair near the window, and as she came toward me, I saw she had a small nurse's cap perched far back on her tightly braided reddish hair.

"I'm Mrs. Parks," she said softly. "Come in here if you want to talk." She drew me back into my room, closing the door behind us. "Sit down." She pushed me into the chair and drew up another beside it. "My, you was sleepin' like a baby. Ain't much more'n a baby, are you?"

"I am eighteen," I told her tartly, "I wish I were twenty-eight!"

She smiled broadly. "An' when you're twenty-eight, you'll be wantin' to be eighteen—folks is never satisfied." Her eyes, small and bright blue, darted around the room. "Not even the folks that live here, an' I guess I'd be satisfied if I had even one room like this, —'stead of forty-five. Even a stick of this furniture an' I'd be set up for life—but my grand-daddy didn't own hisself a mine."

"Uh . . . how is Lina?" I asked hastily, foreseeing reminiscences that might lead me even further from the subject that interested me most.

"Bless you, child, she'll be all right once she gets rested up an' gets to stay in one place. Fancy, Mrs. Fowler tells me she's been on the go for the better part of a month—which is plumb crazy considerin' her condition."

Her comments made me feel worse than ever. In a small voice, I said, "That's my fault. I made her come with me and now . . ." Tears filled my eyes as I remembered the consequences—and Carlo.

"Well, now," Mrs. Parks leaned forward to put a

plump hand on my arm—"how'd you make her come with you, honey? Didn't lasso her by the leg, did you? Didn't put her in irons. . . . In my experience, nobody makes anybody do anythin' they don't want to do."

"Y-you don't understand," I sobbed.

"I understand a whole lot more'n folks give me credit for," she said firmly. She winked at me. "Only I don't let on I do—otherwise, there's a whole lot of interestin' things I wouldn't hear." She looked at me. "My, you're mighty pretty—even prettier'n Virginia Soames, poor thing—an' I like your colorin' a whole lot better. 'Course bein' a redhead myself, I guess I would be more partial to it. She was dark, 'midnight hair' he called it, an' eyes blue as mountain lakes—sure was a shame what happened to her, though. Yes siree, a shame and a disgrace!"

Momentarily diverted from my thoughts, I asked, "Who was Virginia Soames? What did happen to her?"

Mrs. Parks lowered her voice. "Don't let on I said anythin' 'bout her. They wouldn't like it, specially poor George wouldn't. It 'bout done him in. He took on somethin' terrible—can't say as I blame him—after what happened to poor Millie Fairchild. Warn't even two years later. Guess the good Lord don't want him to get hitched—or maybe the right one ain't come his way, yet. Poor George." She sighed.

I was becoming highly interested. "These girls were going to marry Mr. Fowler?"

She nodded solemnly. "Not both at the same time, mind you. Like I said, Millie was two years before— George ain't a Mormon. I had me a patient who was a Mormon once, big strappin' man, like to've made two of me lengthways and sideways. My, he was a big one an' had as nice a little wife as you'd ever want to meet —an' what do you think?" She paused, looking at me out of eyes bright with indignation.

"I—uh—don't know," I said.

"That big galoot went an' proposed to *me!*" She snorted. "I betcha his ears are still ringin' from the boxin' I gave them. Like to've had a relapse before I got through with him. The idea!"

Before I could comment, there was a tap at the door. "Yes?" I said.

The door opened a crack. "Are you awake, miss?" a girl asked in respectful English-accented tones.

"Sure is," Mrs. Parks answered. "You suppose she said 'Yes' in her sleep? C'mon in, Mary."

A thin, pale girl, in a black maid's uniform and white lacy cap, entered carrying a tray on which there was a silver coffee service and two covered dishes. She said, "Good morning, miss. Madame thought you would be wanting breakfast." She set the tray down on a table by the bed.

"Thank you very much," I said.

"You're welcome, I'm sure, miss," she bobbed her head. "Madame says as how your trunks have come from the hotel—they'll be brought up presently."

I had a sudden pang. I had remembered it was Monday and that under other circumstances, I should have been rehearsing for my debut as Nedda. I said faintly, "That's very kind of her."

"Madame also says that when you're ready to come downstairs, you'll find her in the hothouse—you can see it from your window, miss." She walked to the window. "It's that long, low, glass building over there."

I looked. "Yes, I see it. I'll be down pretty soon."

"Very good, miss." Mary bobbed a curtsey and went out.

"English"—Mrs. Parks rolled her eyes—"an' sly as they come. Ever so respectful to your face an' gigglin' fit to kill minute your back is turned. In my opinion, they're just as liable to murder you in your beds as the last lot."

"Murder you . . . ?" I repeated.

Mrs. Parks put her hand over her mouth. "My goodness, I do run on—I'm talkin' far too much. Better get back where I'm supposed to be. You eat your breakfast, honey." Opening the door, she whisked through—if a lady of that girth can be said to whisk. She left me with no less than three unanswered questions—Virginia Soames, Millie Fairchild, and that disturbing reference to murder, which may or may not have ben meaningful. I wanted to follow her, but my eyes fell on the tray at the same time that a whiff of coffee filled my nostrils, and it occurred to me that I was extremely hungry.

The hothouse lay toward the side of the house, not far from the theater. I was admitted by a small man in overalls. The room into which I stepped was hot, moist, and filled with more varieties of orchids than I had ever seen. I was impressed but not overwhelmed by the large yellow, purple, white, spotted, green, and black flowers with their large fleshy petals and strange shapes. Such orchids as I had seen in florist's shops had never appealed to me—I preferred gardenias, carnations, and of course camelias. I did not see Mrs. Fowler immediately, but a second later she emerged from behind a curtain of vines. She was wearing a voluminous blue smock, and there was a smudge of dirt on her cheek. She smiled. "Good morning, my dear. I hope you slept well?"

"Very well," I replied.

"Come along back here." She motioned to the vines, holding them aside as I passed through them to a cleared space where a large metal table stood; on it were more orchid plants. Mrs. Fowler indicated a branch of small white orchids. "They were sick," she said tenderly, "but they're much better now. Shows you what care will do." Her smile broadened. "Guess I could say the same thing about your friend. How's she coming along this morning?"

"She's resting." Dutifully, I said, "Thank you for the lovely breakfast. You're so kind to us."

She held up a protesting hand. "It's what anybody'd do," she said, "and please don't be forever thankin' me. I like to see new faces around here, specially pretty ones. It's been a while since . . . " her face clouded. "But never mind about that. I know you're a singer, my dear, and you'll probably want to practice

—so I'm leaving the theater open for you afternoons. You can go in there any time you please and vocalize to your heart's content with nobody to disturb you. Of course, if you want, you can also use our music room, but I think you'd feel more private in the theater."

"Oh," I said gratefully, "that's awfully good of you!"

"There you go thanking me again. I don't want thanks. Now if you don't mind the heat in here, maybe you'll sit down on this bench and tell me a bit about yourself. You're awful young to be singing professionally, and from what I can see you and your friend are several cuts above the average when it comes to performers . . ."

She listened carefully as I told her about my life until that moment, and when I had concluded, she gave me a long shrewd look. "It's goin' to be hard for you, not performing—just when you'd got your toes wet in it—but you mustn't think life is over. You've a long career ahead of you and all the talent you need—and believe me, I know music. Heard it all over the world. Take it from me, a few months here or there aren't going to make all that difference, no matter what you think."

"But they're going ahead without me, Carlo and the others." I could not help mentioning him, and as I did, tears filled my eyes. Hastily, I blinked them away.

"*Carlo* and the others, eh?" she said. "That dark young man who was glaring at you last night—had a spat with him, did you?"

I looked down. "It—it was all my fault," I whispered. "He can be very kind."

"I'm sure he can be." She nodded. "He seems like a good sort, but all the same he's Eyetalian, and from what I know about them, they've got tempers like geysers, blowing up in all directions—and he's an artist to boot. You don't need another artist in your life, Miss Leila—they have to be parceled out one to a family."

"B-but . . ." I started to cry in earnest; I could not help it.

"But you think you love him. You think you love a

lot of people at eighteen, but that don't mean you do." She smiled at me. "It's a very good thing you're staying on with us . . . might help clear that pretty head."

I did not argue. It would do no good to protest that even though I was merely eighteen, my heart was irretrievably broken and that I felt years older than I had yesterday afternoon in her Shakespearean garden, when Carlo had kissed me. I only sighed.

She patted my shoulder. "Such a long sigh, poor girlie. You'll get over it, sure as shooting." For a moment, her bright eyes grew somber. "You've no idea what you can get over in this life. And as for them going on without you—one door closes and another opens. Now, you're going to have a bit of time on your hands for the nonce and you can't practice all the day, so I want you to feel right at home. There's the library —got a heap of books in there. Old Fowler—that's the first George, I mean—bought 'em in sets when he had the place built. Collected a lot of first editions, too, 'cause he'd heard it was the thing to do—not because he ever looked at much besides the newspapers—so there're plenty of books. Do you ride?"

"I used to ride at home," I told her.

"Course you would, being a Westerner like me. I'm from Sacramento, too. My folks came to California about the same time old Fowler did, only they didn't make their money out of mining—made it off the miners, instead. Had themselves a saloon. It was a wicked place." She frowned. "There's always wickedness where there's money—two of them go hand in hand, and if you don't pay the piper one year, he'll get you the next." She stared moodily at the table. "Yep, he always gets you in the end." She gave herself a little shake. "But that don't concern you. What I really wanted to tell you is we got a stableful of horses. George'd be pleased as punch if you'd like to ride—him an' Kezia go nearly every morning."

"Oh," I said, thinking of Kezia Graves as I had seen her the previous night near the elevator, "I wouldn't want to intrude . . . "

Mrs. Fowler made her habitual gesture of holding up her hand. "Don't you be put off by her," she said. "Just don't pay her any mind. She don't run this house, I do." She added quickly, "She's a good enough girl in her way, but she's prickly like a scared porcupine, shooting out her quills and asking questions afterward." She pursed her mouth. "You'd think that after all these years . . . But never mind—just you remember what I told you, and if you want to go riding, just say so."

"I don't have a habit," I said.

"I've got a whole heap—and though I'm bigger all 'round than you, I think with a few nips and tucks you could fit into my clothes. What's your shoe size?"

"Four."

"Mine's four and a half." She smiled at me. "Larger's better'n smaller—so you'll have yourself an outfit. And meanwhile there's tennis and croquet. I'm good at croquet and I get sick of beating everybody. Like to take on somebody new for a change. By the way, dinner's usually served at one and supper at seven—hope that's not too late for you."

"It's fine," I said.

"Well, you're an accommodating sort of a girl. I like you. Liked you the first moment I set eyes on you. I think we're going to get along very well—and you just make yourself at home, here at the Thumb."

That startled me. "The—the Thumb?"

She laughed. "Now don't tell me you haven't heard about the "Sore Thumb"?

"I—had—heard . . . "

"Bless you, child, don't be embarrassed. Everybody calls it that, and it's a good name for it, too. It *does* stick out like a sore thumb. Old Fowler had it built according to his specifications, and they was that it had to be big and look like some of the places he'd seen when he was sailing the seven seas. So we got Moorish and Gothic and Norman all in one bundle—which is bad enough, but it might've been worse. Supposing he'd also been partial to igloos?"

I had to laugh. "But the furniture is lovely," I said.

"I guess I can take credit for that," she said in a pleased voice. "For the furniture and the paintings. You should've seen what he had in this big barn when I came here." She groaned. "Most of it was horsehair and dark, and so I reared back and said I wasn't going to live in a house that looked like a mausoleum inside and out. George, Jr., went along with me, and the old man was on his last legs by then and couldn't say a thing. Besides, he wouldn't've had any call to complain on account of I used my own money. Had myself a heap of fun—I wasn't much older than you in those days, and George, Jr., was around. It was a different place, then. Wasn't a night we didn't entertain—days, too, with picnics, riding, mountain-climbing. Sure had ourselves a time until George, Jr., up and cashed in his checks." The somber look had returned to her eyes. "Young man, too, wasn't more'n thirty-five. That's twins for you—didn't survive his sister for more'n a year." She smiled wryly. "Heavens, I didn't mean to chop off such a large chunk of family history. . . . You look like you're about to wilt in this place—better get some fresh air, and I'd better get back to the Cybidium Alexandrei, here."

When I emerged from the hothouse, I was surprised to find that my hair was wet and my dress damp. I had not really noticed the heat—I had been too interested in talking, or rather listening, to Mrs. Fowler, who in addition to being one of the kindest people I had ever met, was also one of the more puzzling. Though she spoke in a slangy twang, she was obviously cultured; and though most of the furnishings I had seen in the house were in excellent taste, she had chosen to wear red silk and diamonds the previous night—a combination Mama would not have hesitated to pronounce "dreadful." Perhaps the late George, Jr., had advised her on the furnishings. I wondered about him and his twin sister, who had died so early—though thirty-four or -five was not all that young. It was middle-aged— but still I should not like to die at thirty-four, especially if I were as rich as the Fowlers. Rich on both sides, it seemed. I recalled her remark about "paying the piper." What had she meant? And that odd reference to a "pretty face" broken off mid-sentence. Had she been talking about Virginia Soames or Millie Fairchild? I really wanted to know more about those two mysterious girls. I was half-inclined to go back upstairs to Mrs. Parks, but it was very pleasant in the gardens. A cool breeze was blowing, and on turning, I caught a glimpse of blue water behind a hedge and decided to do a little exploring before I went in. Circling the hedge, I found an opening, and on passing through it, I came upon a wide round pool, centered by a statue of frightened Europa clinging to the back of a charging bull. Its reflection, mirrored in that still water, unfortunately reminded me of the drowned Ophelia in the Shakespearean garden, and I relived the moment when Carlo had taken me in his arms—Carlo, whom I might never see again! Sobbing, I sank down on the grass. I cried for a long time. I cried until my head throbbed and my eyes ached.

"Miss MacKenzie! What's the matter? You—you're not hurt, are you?"

Hands were on my shoulders. I looked up into the anxious face of George Fowler. "No—no, it—it's just that I was unhappy over . . . "

"Over Miss Da Costa?" he questioned. "That's good." He flushed, "I—uh—mean I—I'm glad you're not hurt or anything. I thought . . . well, it doesn't matter what I thought. You're all right."

Despite my grief, his apparent relief intrigued me. Why had he believed me hurt? Obviously, I could not ask him. I said, "I was upset over Lina. She—she's dreadfully ill."

His smile was reassuring. "Mrs. Parks is looking after her, which means she's in very good hands. The best."

"That's good to know." I sniffed and brushed a hand over my eyes.

"Here," he said, producing a handkerchief that he

pressed into my hand. "Linen is more effective than flesh when it comes to drying tears."

"Thank you." I wiped my eyes and cheeks. "I don't usually cry," I told him, feeling embarrassed.

"It's quite understandable." He sat down beside me on the grass. "You know, Miss MacKenzie, I was close to crying myself last night, when our dance was so quickly interrupted."

"Oh!" I had to smile. "I—don't believe it."

"It's true," he said solemnly. "I've seldom had a partner that suited me so well—it was like holding a feather in my arms.'

"You're very kind," I said. "I enjoyed it, too."

"Did you?" He looked at me intently.

His scrutiny made me feel nervous. "You dance well," I said.

"Not always." He continued to eye me intently. "It depends on my partner."

"Oh." Even to my own ears, my trill of laughter seemed forced. "You're only being polite. I'm sure there must be many ladies who dance as well as I do —or much better." I looked down, knowing I was blushing. It would be useless to deny that despite my unhappiness over the loss of Carlo, I was pleased by George Fowler's evident admiration. He was, I decided, even more handsome than I remembered, for in addition to his uncanny resemblance to Lord Byron, he was extremely well-built—broad-shouldered, slim-waisted, and at least a head taller than Carlo. A memory of what Mrs. Fowler and Lina had said about the inconstancy of eighteen smote me. I rose abruptly. "I must get back to Lina!" I exclaimed.

"Must you?" He got to his feet. "But she's in very good hands, as I told you."

"Still, if she's awake, she will wonder where I am. I should be there."

"You take your responsibilities very seriously," he observed. "I like that."

"She's been very good to me," I replied, wondering

what he would have thought had he heard my discussion with Carlo last night.

He accompanied me back to the house. "Are you comfortable?" he inquired, as we approached the side door which, he said, opened directly onto the staircase.

"How could anyone not be comfortable, here?" I asked. "It's so beautiful!"

"Um." His mouth twisted. "Beauty is as beauty does." Opening the door, he said, "The Rose Suite is the second door on your left at the head of the stairs. We'll see you at dinner, I hope?"

"Yes, I shall be there." I smiled.

As I hurried up the stairs, I almost prayed Mrs. Parks would be in a mood to answer my questions—at least some of them. At least she could tell me about Virginia Soames and Millie Fairchild—the others would be a little more difficult to answer and equally difficult to phrase. How could I ask her, "What did he mean by beauty is as beauty does? Why were his eyes so somber and his mouth so grim when he said it? Why did he think I had been hurt? Did all of his unhappiness stem from his two lost loves? Why had there been only two? A man like that—handsome, charming, wealthy—should have been able to find consolation. Why hadn't he?" No, I could not ask her those questions. I should have to be content with such information as I could obtain about the girls.

When I reached Lina's door, I found it ajar and heard her talking weakly to Mrs. Parks. Should I say that I was delighted to find her awake and more responsive than she had been the night before? No, I must be honest and admit that I had craved enlightment and was sorry it would have to be postponed.

Lina still looked very frail, but she was so glad to see me that my uneasy conscience pricked me anew. "Oh, Lina," I said, meaning it now, "I'm so glad you're awake. You seem better!"

"I—think I am . . . a little," she whispered. "Where've you been?"

"Walking."

She smiled. "It's good for you to walk. Such a lovely place—such a lovely room."

"Whyn't you sit down, honey?" Mrs. Parks pulled a chair up to the side of the bed.

"Thank you," I said, taking it. "It *is* a lovely room. Mine is, too. Mrs. Fowler tells me she furnished the house."

"She did, too," Mrs. Parks affirmed. "Every stick. Sold off all the stuff old George'd accumulated—junk, that was. Lot've folks bought it, though—them as wasn't afraid to give it house room."

"Afraid?" Lina and I said together.

"Oh"—Mrs. Parks bit her lip—"there I go again, talkin' outa turn. Oh, well, I don't see no harm in tellin' you about it—it's common knowledge, after all. You see, George Fowler was such a mean cuss—used to call him 'foul Fowler' behind his back—that folks 'round here'd have it anythin' comin' outa the Thumb was unlucky."

" 'Unlucky . . . ' That's what our driver said," Lina murmured. "He said they were unlucky."

"Well, they sure have been," Mrs. Parks responded. "Leastways, they ain't had as much good from the money as they could've, what with old George havin' an apoplectic stroke an' livin' out his days paralyzed from head to toe. Only thing he could still move was his eyes, an' I heard tell the look in them was enough to shrivel your gizzard!"

"Oh"—Lina shuddered—"poor man! I hope he didn't live long in such a condition."

"Lived a sight longer'n he'd've wanted, I'll bet," Mrs. Parks replied. "Twelve years!"

"Twelve years." Lina gasped.

"Folks said as how it was a judgment on him.' Mrs. Parks lowered her voice. "Don't let on I told you, but old George's supposed to've stole his minin' claim from a Mexican feller, who up an' drunk hisself to death an' died cussin' old George an' all his kin—said as how none of 'em would get any good from the money. Seemed like he spoke true."

A glint of amusement flickered in Lina's sunken eyes. "More superstition," she whispered. "Lots of great fortunes have been founded on thievery, and plenty of millionaires have enjoyed their wealth up to the very last minute."

"That's sure as spittin'," Mrs. Parks agreed, "but the Fowlers have been unlucky, no two ways about it. Old George's wife, pretty little thing she was, wouldn't say boo to a goose an' was scared to death of him—anyhow she died in childbed, which is no wonder since she birthed two husky twins. Then the two of them died within a year of each other. Julie Fowler was beaten to death by her husband."

"Beaten to death!" Again Lina and I had spoken in unison.

"Beaten to death," Mrs. Parks repeated with a melancholy relish. "Poor little thing! He was crazy of course, jealous of everythin' an' everybody—with no cause nohow—on account of she upped'n run off with him. Got disinherited for her pains, even though her brother kept on helpin' her out, on account of Elihu Graves was too busy sneakin' around spyin' on Julie to be much use as a doctor. Anyhow, he was crazy as a coot. Had notions about doctorin' like you wouldn't believe. Said as how sickness was mostly in the head—guess he meant hisself, 'cause he had to be stark ravin' crazy, wallopin' her like he did. Broke her all to pieces an' lit out for parts unknown. Died a couple years afterward in Mexico. He's out there in the family plot, buried next to George an' Julie. George, Jr., wouldn't've wanted that, but he didn't have no say in the matter—Julie's dyin' killed him, too. Twelve months later, they was lyin' side by side with a tombstone between 'em—a mornin' angel in marble. George, Jr., was mighty partial to marble."

"Did he put that statue in the Shakespearean garden

—the Ophelia in the water?" I asked with a reminiscent shudder.

"That drowned piece?" Mrs. Parks inquired.

"Yes."

"Yep, that was his idea. Mrs. Fowler never liked it much, but Julie was crazy for it—an' anythin' she wanted, he did. They was mighty close until she married. He didn't get married until a couple of years later."

I could not imagine anyone liking the statue of drowned Ophelia. Somehow it made me feel less sympathetic toward the late Julie Fowler Graves. Graves! "Was Julie Kezia's mother?" I asked.

"That's right, only you'd never know it. Kezia Graves don't look nothin' like Julie—nor her father neither, for that matter. Elihu Graves was a handsome man." She flushed. "Not that Kezia ain't got her points, but she favors old George too much—specially 'round the eyes."

"That was evident from the portrait we saw," Lina murmured. "Was she very young when her mother died?"

"She was . . . well, she's twenty-seven, now, so she must've been nigh on eight years old."

"Old enough to know what was happening, poor little girl." Lina leaned back wearily among her pillows.

Mrs. Parks gave her a sharp glance. "You're plumb tuckered out, ain't you? Guess we've been doin' too much talkin'."

"No," Lina told her, "I've been interested. Isn't anybody ever happy in this life?" She sighed.

"I am," Mrs. Parks said cheerfully. "I've always enjoyed every minute of livin'—always said no matter what happens, I'm glad the good Lord put me here on this earth right now. Why, when you stop to think about it, it's all so interestin'. What with folks being' able to talk to each other without havin' to stir a step beyond their own front doors, an' then we don't need to mess 'round with gaslights no more—electricity's better an' cleaner—an' pretty soon we won't need to stall an' feed a horse 'count've you'll have an automobile'n they say that pretty soon they'll be goin' faster'n any race horse, an' maybe we'll all be flyin' through the air before we're done!"

Lina smiled at her. "I like you, Mrs. Parks!" she exclaimed.

The nurse loked down at her fondly. "Well, that just goes double, honey, an' to prove it, I'm goin' to have you up an' around in no time, see if I don't. But meanwhile you got to rest some more. Try an' sleep if you can. Later, I'll have them fix up a real nice tray for you."

"Oh, I couldn't eat anything," Lina protested feebly.

"You could swallow some broth, honey."

There was a tap at the door. "Yes?" Mrs. Parks called.

Mary appeared on the threshold between the two rooms. "If you please, miss," she said to me, "I've brought you your dinner."

"Dinner?" I was startled. "I thought I should be having it with the family."

"Miss Kezia sent it up to you, miss," Mary replied. "She said you'd probably want to be near your friend."

"That was real thoughtful of her!" Mrs. Parks exclaimed in accents of surprise.

A jolt of disappointment went through me, and I realized I had been looking forward to dinner with the Fowlers. A split second later, I also realized that mother and son had specifically invited me to come—invitations of which Kezia Graves might not have been aware. I decided to act on that supposition. I said, "Tell Miss Graves that I do appreciate her thoughtfulness, but since Miss Lina wishes to rest now, I might as well join the family in the dining room, as Mrs. Fowler requested."

A variety of expressions chased across Mary's face. She looked startled, concerned, and almost frightened when she answered, "B-but I've brought the tray up here."

"Surely you can take it back down," I said sweetly. "Perhaps Miss Graves was unaware of Mrs. Fowler's invitation."

Mary's face had become impassive again. "Yes, miss." She bobbed her usual curtsey. "Very good, miss." She hurried out, closing the door behind her.

"Well, if that don't beat the Dutch!"

I turned to find Mrs. Parks staring at me out of round eyes. "What?" I demanded belligerently. Now that I had made my stand, I was beginning to have second thoughts about it.

"It never occurred to me. I thought she was doin' it outa kindness, but one look at Mary an' I knew I was dead wrong—she was bein' pure cussed mean. Kezia Graves, I'm talkin' about—an' that's more like her, I can tell you. She's got more'n looks in common with old George."

"I don't understand," Lina said.

"It's this way, miss. Ever since she's come of age, she's been bound an' determined to run the household. For a while, Mrs. Fowler let her have her head, but she got so persnickety that she pulled the reins in on her—'count've nobody's goin' to order Aurelia Fowler around! But she still tries, an' she don't cotton much to strangers. Never has. Nor did old George, from what I've heard tell." She grinned. "But you sure put her nose outa joint. Yes, ma'am, you sure did!"

Notwithstanding Mrs. Parks's outspoken admiration, I felt nervous when I made my way to the dining room, which was in the main part of the building to the right of the stairs. I arrived a little before the appointed hour, and again was overwhelmed by the grandeur of my surroundings. It was a long narrow chamber with four tall windows, all facing the gardens; two of its entrances opened on the corridor and a third led into a large butler's pantry. The walls were covered with a fine scarlet damask on which hung a number of lovely landscapes in heavy gold frames. A crystal chandelier descended from a sculptured plaster ceiling, and on either side of a long polished table were tall brass lamps which appeared to be East Indian in origin. Also East Indian in design if not origin was a mammoth silver centerpiece representing a huge palm tree supporting some twenty candles. Below these, two silver Indian hunters chased a sleek silver tiger with emerald eyes. The table, I noticed, was set for three.

I was trying to decide whether to go or stay when Mrs. Fowler entered. Her eyes widened as she saw me. "Hello, girlie, I'm mighty glad you decided to join us after all!" she said effusively.

I gave her a look of what I hoped was effectively simulated surprise. "But you invited me. At least that was my understanding."

She gave me a piercing look. "I was told you'd made plans to dine upstairs with Miss Da Costa."

"Oh, no," I said. "Lina's still resting. I hope you don't mind that I sent the tray back. I thought there'd been some sort of a misunderstanding and I didn't want you to think I was rude."

Mrs. Fowler smiled broadly. "I don't mind in the least," she told me, "and I'm sure there was a misunderstanding." Her bright eyes bored into mine. "You've got spunk, girlie. I said it last night and I say it again!" Glancing past me, she added, "Good afternoon, Kezia."

"Good afternoon, Aunt Aurelia," Miss Graves said in accents chill enough to vitiate her greeting. She was wearing a blue linen dress that set off her dull coloring better than anything else I had seen her wear and she had dressed her brown hair with care, but if her attire was more becoming, her expression was not—her brown eyes glittered with anger.

Fastening them on me, she seemed about to speak, but before she opened her mouth, I said quickly, "It was so good of you to send me that tray, Miss Graves. I do appreciate it, but since Mrs. Fowler had specified that I come to dinner, I thought I'd better do so."

"And I'm glad she did," Mrs. Fowler said.

"Oh, you're here!" George Fowler exclaimed from the threshold. "Kezia told me . . . "

Kezia Graves's anger faded. With a little deprecating laugh, she said, "I made a mistake, George. Your mother had already invited Miss MacKenzie to dine with us."

"We'd both already invited her, then." He turned to me. "How is Miss Da Costa?"

"She seems better," I relaxed—the uncomfortable moment had passed, and it did not return during the meal. Mrs. Fowler wanted to hear about my debut and even Kezia Graves seemed interested. I am afraid I talked too much, and certainly I ate too much of fish in cream sauce, breast of chicken in gravy, roast beef, beets, stringbeans, cheese soufflé, salad, sherbert, cakes, and coffee, all beautifully prepared and served on the finest china by a maid Mrs. Fowler addressed as Agnes and Bartram, the butler.

As we were finishing our coffee, Mrs. Fowler said to her son, "You going out to the groves this afternoon?"

He nodded. "Kezia and I had planned on it." He looked at me, "Would you like to come, Miss MacKenzie?"

Out of the corner of my eye, I saw Kezia, who was sitting next to me, turn rigid. Deciding that I had provoked her enough for one day, I answered, "Not this afternoon, thank you. I'd like to be near Lina, if you don't mind."

"I do mind," he replied, "but there will be other afternoons."

Meeting his eyes, I read in them an unmistakable interest. I looked away quickly. "You're very kind," I murmured, praying that I did not look too pleased. I was heartily glad when I could leave the table—I needed to be alone.

Yet, when I had achieved my purpose, I actually felt regretful that I would not be seeing "Lord Byron," as I still called him, that afternoon. Thinking of my nickname, I wondered if there were quite as much of a resemblance as I had imagined. There was one way of finding out—surely they would have a Collected Works in the library.

However, when I came into the library and found myself confronting four long high walls covered with books, I despaired of ever finding my Byron. I was about to leave when I saw the portrait of a young woman in a white dress hanging over the fireplace in the center of the room. A closer glance showed me a face that was neither beautiful nor striking, but the features were pleasant and the gray eyes full of intelligence. With a slight shock, I realized I was looking at Mrs. Fowler as she must appeared some thirty years back. On turning away, I saw two more portraits in the recesses between the shelves across the room—one of them was that of a young man with a sweep of brown hair and steady blue eyes. His nose was straight, his mouth firm, though a little thin. There was a slight cleft in his pointed chin and I remembered that I had noticed a similar cleft in George Fowler's chin—this was probably his father; when I saw the portrait in the next recess, I was sure of it, for here was the same face only cast in feminine form—the outlines softer and a mass of wavy chesnut hair piled on top of the well-shaped head. Yes, here was Julie Fowler, disinherited by her father, murdered by her husband—but when the picture had been painted, those long shadows had not yet fallen across her path. There was a roguish gleam in her large blue eyes, and she might even have been flirting with the artist—certainly he had lavished more care on her portrait than on that of her brother. As I looked at her charming, impudent little face, it seemed incredible to me that she had borne a daughter like Kezia; they could have had very little in common!

Moving around the room, I looked for other portraits but found none. I also searched through several shelves hoping to find my Byron, but it eluded me. However, on a desk, I discovered something that interested me almost as much—a thick, fat volume covered in scarlet velvet and gold-stamped with the words "Family Album."

Seizing it, I settled down on the couch and opened it eagerly. At first I was disappointed to find only tintypes of hard-eyed men and women posed stiffly in the "Sunday-best" of some fifty-odd years ago. However, midway through, I found some yellowed photographs of "Old" George Fowler, looking even less prepossessing than in his portrait. The more revealing camera had caught the cunning expression in the eyes—I could well imagine he had cheated and robbed that hapless Mexican miner—and he appeared capable of any sort of skullduggery. In one of the photographs there was a young woman standing behind him, a tremulous smile on her lips, her eyes wide and frightened. Though she had her hand on his shoulder, it seemed to me she touched it but tentatively, as if with the click of the camera, she would have immediately removed it and fled. Even if she had not resembled the twins, I would have known her as goose-shy Melissa. On another page, there was a picture of two babies in identical long dresses and white bonnets—the twins; later, they appeared in sailor suits, and a final picture of the pair showed them aged ten or thereabouts, both with the same toothless gap in their grin. It was the last time Julie appeared in the album, though there were other views of George, Jr., in various stages of development —from a lanky fourteen-year-old in a striped bathing dress to a tall young man on what must have been the Grand Tour, since it showed him against the background of a Roman ruin. Later, he stood with his arm around a girl who was not Mrs. Fowler and another who was—she looked so happy that my heart ached for her. There were photos of the wedding, and later the couple was shown on horseback, at a campfire, and in company with other people. A baby on a fur rug was probably George, III, and there the album ended, leaving me wondering whether the older Julie had been camera-shy, or whether, in addition to disinheriting her, her angered father had expunged her from the family album. It was a depressing thought—indeed, the whole story of Julie Fowler was depressing. I did not want to think about her. I had my own troubles, and as I gazed around the room, these came flooding back on me again. It had been on this very couch that Lina had lain the night before, and in my mind's eye, I saw Carlo's furious glance as he beckoned me to follow him. Again I remembered my foolish futile outburst, again I saw the disgust in his dark eyes and knew I had lost him—and with him, my chance of singing in San Francisco in the spring. Why had I come back into the library, scene of all that anguish? Then, with a slight start, I remembered exactly why I had come—to find a picture of Lord Byron, which brought me full-circle to George Fowler, in whose glance I had read only admiration, suggesting that if I did not please a certain temperamental Italian conductor, there were other men with other ideas. Furthermore, there were also other opera companies in the world! Angrily, I muttered under my breath, "And I will sing in them, Signor Carlo Benedetto—I shall not only sing but I shall triumph!"

Defiantly, I stalked out of the library, down the corridor, and into the gardens. Though I had only been there once, I had no trouble finding the theater, and as Mrs. Fowler had promised, the door was open and a light was on. I went to the piano and began to play Nedda's music—it soothed me as nothing else could have done. The unhappiness of the previous day vanished. I forgot, too, the Fowlers and their strange, unhappy history—yes, even George. I was aware only of my art.

I vocalized for at least two hours, then, as I started out of the building, I saw a shadow on the threshold—someone was standing just outside the door. I smiled to myself—I had drawn an audience. When I came out, I found John, the tall footman who had carried Lina to her room. He was standing there, motionless, his face registering no expression. I might have pleased him or he might have hated it—I could not tell. I said, "Good afternoon, John."

He did not answer me; he turned and walked away. I hoped it was not a critical comment. Probably, I decided, he was embarrassed at having been discovered.

The house was very quiet when I returned. There were no servants about, and in most of the rooms the draperies were drawn against the sun. Upstairs, I found Lina asleep and Mrs. Parks dozing in her chair. She opened her eyes when I appeared at the threshold, but any hopes of another enlightening conversation were dashed when she said in a low voice, "My gosh, what're you doin' up an' around? It's siesta time now."

"Siesta time?"

"That's right—everybody takes a snooze 'round here an' don't get up until four or five. It's an old Spanish custom—good one, too." Leaning back in her chair, she closed her eyes. "Yes sireebob, it's a good one."

Taking the hint, I withdrew. I was not particularly tired, but since there was nothing else to do, I took Mrs. Parks's advice and lay down. I did not think I would sleep; as usual I was wrong. When I opened my eyes again, the sky had darkened and the clouds were rosy in the setting sun. A glance at the little golden clock on my mantelpiece informed me that it was six! I had slept nearly three hours. Slipping out of bed, I peered into Lina's room. She was awake, but Mrs. Parks had gone—instead, there was a dark woman in a gaily colored cotton dress in her place. Lina smiled and motioned to me. "This is Mrs. Sanchez," she explained. "She stays here at night."

"Mrs. Parks has gone home?" I inquired.

"She left at five."

I stifled a sigh. Resolutely, I banished Virginia Soames and Millie Fairchild from my thoughts as I asked, "Are you feeling better, Lina?"

"My breath's a bit easier," she acknowledged.

A faint hope stirred in me—perhaps . . . But looking at her wan face and darkly circled eyes, I knew that even if she rested for a week, she would not be ready to travel with me again. Perhaps she could never accompany me, perhaps . . . I was suddenly ashamed of myself. Sinking down on the end of her bed, I began to tell Lina about the house.

The rest of the evening was uneventful. At Lina's request, I supped with her in her room, which must have pleased Kezia Graves. I went to bed early that night and awakened at dawn on Tuesday morning to the sound of rain beating against my windowpanes. On rising, I found huge swollen rainclouds overhead, and rather than mere drops, veritable sheets of water seemed to be pouring out of the heavens. Judging from the look of that lowering sky, the rain could continue all day—which meant I should be housebound, which meant, too, that a lot of other people would not venture into country lanes that would be thick mud by midmorning, which meant that the Sacramento Theater would certainly not be filled to capacity that night, which meant that even if I had sung Nedda, I might have performed in a largely empty house. A further vision of streaming streets, dank dressing rooms, sodden clothing, and possibly leaking ceilings arose to cheer me.

"Serves him right!" I muttered vindictively.

I breakfasted in my room, a proceeding I did not regret. In spite of such solace as I could find in the contemplation of the company's plight, I was still in a bad mood, and I did not need it aggravated by Kezia Graves glowering at me across a table.

It was close to eight when I tentatively opened Lina's door. To my relief, Mrs. Sanchez had gone and Mrs. Parks, starched and fresh-looking, sat by the bed. On seeing me, she put a plump finger to her lips. "Sleepin'," she whispered, and tiptoeing from her chair, she followed me into the other room. "My, my, my, ain't it weather for ducks!" she exclaimed, looking into the drowned gardens.

"Does it rain like this much?" I asked.

"Cats an' dogs in the fall," she said. "It'd make Noah feel right at home. There's times when they got to use boats on the streets of Sacramento—water up to here!"

She pointed to the ceiling. "An' it looks like this might be one of them days, yep, that's the way it looks."

"Dear me," I said, "they mightn't be able to give a performance tonight at all. The opera company, I mean."

"Bless you, honey, if it keeps on the way it's goin', they won't be able to do nothin' all week—that there theater will be flooded to the roof!"

"Gracious!" I clicked my tongue. To say that I rejoiced over the possible routing of the company would be an exaggeration, but that I was not as distressed as I might be was, alas, quite true. I could not resist a glance around my luxurious quarters—if I had to be indoors, I would rather be here than in the small rooms Lina and I had shared at the hotel.

"You oughta be glad you're here." Mrs. Parks's inadvertent voicing of my own thoughts caused me to start slightly. "You have a pleasant meal yesterday? Dinnertime, I mean?"

Meeting her curious glance, I had to smile. No wonder she was so full of information, certainly she did not scruple to demand it. "Very pleasant," I said. "Once Miss Graves realized there'd been a misunderstanding."

"Misunderstanding!" Mrs. Parks snorted. "Always was a nasty piece, that one."

"Her mother was very pretty. I saw her picture in the library."

"Prettier even than the picture. I seen her when I was a slip of a girl. Always had a pleasant word for everybody, but her daughter don't know you're alive. 'Ceptin' for Mrs. Fowler and George, she ain't even got a pleasant look for you. Them eyes—like two burnt holes in a blanket! But I suppose if I'd seen my father beat up on my mother like she done, might've turned me queer, too. She didn't hardly speak none at all when she first come her—just went around like she was practically deaf an' dumb."

"She saw her mother and father . . . " I shuddered. "How terrible."

"Yep, terrible. Heard tell as she was right in the

room when it happened. Tried to run in front of her mother an' got knocked silly for her pains."

"Oh! How dreadful!"

"Yeah," Mrs. Parks nodded. "It gave her bad nightmares—they say the first years she was here, she'd walk in her sleep an' wake up screamin' fit to kill."

Much as I did not like her, I felt sorry for Kezia Graves. "I'm glad there were people who could care for her."

"Yep, she was lucky, there—'bout the only thing lucky ever happen to her, I guess—but I don't know as it was 'specially lucky for the rest of 'em. Looks like they got her on their hands permanent. Don't look like she's goin' to get married."

"Hasn't there ever been anyone?" I asked."

"Seems to me there was a couple when she was younger, but she never give'em no tumble. Maybe after what her father done she's scared of men. . . . " Mrs. Parks pulled a solemn face. "Maybe I would be, too."

"She doesn't seem afraid of Mr. Fowler," I said.

"No, she's crazy about *him*. They always been more like brother an' sister'n cousins. I guess that's only natural—her mother and his father bein' twins an' all. Yeah, she's fond of him, all right—took it near as bad as he done when all that trouble happened over Millie Fairchild—an' then Virginia Soames less'n two years later. They say bad things don't happen singly an' they sure haven't here."

At last, she had broached the subject I most wanted to discuss and I had not even had to prompt her! "What did happen?" I asked, trying not to sound too eager.

The gleam in Mrs. Parks's eyes suggested that if I was eager to hear the story, she was no less eager to tell it, but she heaved a long lugubrious sigh. "Oh, it was awful. Guess I shouldn't bring it all up again, but it ain't no secret. Not around these parts. Everybody was so sorry for him, him bein' so handsome an' all. That Millie Fairchild! She tried to make up to him afterward, tried somethin' awful, but of course, he wouldn't even speak to her. Whole county was on hand when it happened—Mrs. Fowler was like to sink through the floor, I'll bet."

"When *what* happened?" I demanded, trying to quell my impatience.

"Left him at the altar," she said. "Right smack at the altar. There she was in her weddin' dress—made a beautiful bride, so I've been told. She was blonde like him with big blue eyes, an' the church packed to the gills with people. Like I said, 'most the county was there an' she's comin' up the aisle on her father's arm an' George standin' near the preacher with the best man an' the organ is playin' the weddin' march, an' all of a sudden, she turns an' hightails it outa there like all the devils in hell was chasin' her. Jumps in her father's carriage an' tells the driver to take her home. How do you like that?"

"Why did she do it?" I cried.

"Got some sorta bee in her bonnet"—Mrs. Parks raised her eyebrows—"on account've the next day she changed her mind back an' come here with her father, carryin' on fit to kill an' sayin' as how she didn't know what got into her. But of course by that time it was too late, 'cause George was hurt real bad an' he wouldn't even see her. He an' his mother an' Kezia took off for Europe, three four days later, an' didn't come back for a whole year!"

"She must have been crazy!" I exclaimed.

"That's what Mrs. Fowler an' Kezia said—'specially since Millie practically went into a decline. Kept writin' to George an' beggin' him to see her, right up until he got engaged to poor Virginia Soames."

"Did she leave him at the altar, too?"

"Nope, never got the chance. She was murdered."

"M-murdered?" I stuttered. "H-how?"

"Choked to death. Down in the gardens, it happened, in one of the summerhouses—wooden one, it's all shut up now. Don't guess they'll ever want to open it again. It's a pity, it was a real pretty place—all the walls was hand-painted."

The fate of the summer house did not interest me.

"Who killed her?" I asked impatiently. "Did they ever find out?"

"Oh, yes, one of the gardeners saw him runnin' away. It was a Mexican boy, worked in the kitchen. They had all Mexican help, then, an' they fired the lot of 'em. 'Course, that didn't bring poor Virginia Soames back. Oh, there was some to-do over that, an' George Fowler took to his bed—he was sick maybe six weeks. Can't say's I blame him, specially after Millie an' all. Does seem to be a sort of judgment on 'em, don't it? Sins of the fathers, like it says in the Bible."

"But it was Virginia Soames who was killed," I reminded her.

"Guilt by association," Mrs. Parks intoned solemnly. "Guess it'll be a long time before George Fowler gets up enough gumption to go courtin' again."

"I—uh guess so," I said, remembering our encounters yesterday. I also recalled his reaction when he found me on the grass. Taken in context with Mrs. Parks's story, his alarm was easily understandable. Had he expected to find me dead? I shivered slightly—of a sudden, I was not quite as excited by the flattering interest he had taken in me. Not that I believed in judgments, but didn't disasters come in threes? Of course, Lina would have termed that a mere superstition, but . . .

"S'pose I'd better get back to my patient." Mrs. Parks rose with a creak of linen. "You won't let on I told you none of this?"

"Never," I assured her.

After she left me, I went slowly back to the window and stared into the gardens. With their wind-lashed trees, their muddy paths, their statuary—ghostly white against the dun-colored sky—they had taken on a sinister aspect. In fact, the whole house seemed sinister and forbidding. It was quite easy to imagine that all who dwelt within its walls were accursed.

Gripped by this sentiment, I took out my journal and settled down to record all that had happened during the—was it only two days I had been there? By the time I had finished writing, my initial trepidation had, however, vanished, and with it my fears about family curses, for on due reflection I recalled that my own mother had been twice widowed without even the benefit of a sinful grandfather or a purloined fortune! Then there was poor Lina with her shattered career, and as for myself—I forebore to dwell on heartaches largely of my own making. Instead, as Mama had always enjoined me to do, I decided I would try not to think of myself at all. I would endeavor to be useful to poor Lina—perhaps I could read to her or maybe she would have a chore I might perform.

My spirits were entirely restored as I went toward her room. It was really quite uplifting to think of others besides yourself. Alas for my good intentions—a glance inside showed me that she was still asleep, which left me with nothing to do. It was then I remembered the music room; Mrs. Fowler had said I might use it, and since it was the habit of the household to rest during the afternoon, I decided it would be more considerate to practice that morning.

There were two servants at work in the hall when I came down. A man was polishing the banisters and a maid was scrubbing the floor; both stopped in their work and stared at me with curious and, to my mind, unfriendly glances, though what I might have done to merit their disapproval, I could not imagine nor did I care. Coolly, I said, "Could you tell me where the music room is, please?"

The maid nodded. "It's directly down the corridor, miss. Last door on your right."

"Thank you," I said. On leaving the hall, I heard a burst of snickering accompanied by a harsher guffaw, bringing to mind Mrs. Parks's dictum concerning British servants in general and Mary in particular. It seemed to be true—which should not have bothered me, but it did. I could not see why I should be an object of amusement to anyone. Perhaps it was my connection with the theater, a profession many people still held in anathema? At any rate, it did not matter! Angrily,

I pulled open the designated door and then all my irritation magically dissipated as I stepped into yet another lovely chamber.

It was not grand like the ballroom or impressive like the dining room, but despite wide windows facing the rainwashed garden and dismal sky, it seemed filled with sunshine. This extraordinary effect was created by the most exquisite wallpaper—no, on closer examination, wall *paintings*—panel after panel depicting delicate bushes abloom with rare, exotic flowers in harmonious colors, feathery trees, crystaline waterfalls, classic pillars under a vivid blue sky. At first, I stared at these, entranced, hardly glancing at the furnishings, but then I noticed a golden harp in one corner of the room and in the other a grand piano with a gilded body and painted cover—closer examination revealed its white keys to be mother of pearl and the black seemed to be onyx! It was so very grand that I hesitated to touch it. Turning away from it, I found myself looking into a mirror. To my utter horror, the end of my nose was quite blue! When writing, I must have rubbed it with an inky finger. I glanced at my hands. Yes, there was ink on my fingers. I blushed. "Oh, dear," I said out loud, "that's why they laughed."

"Why who laughed?"

"Oooooh," I squealed, leaping backward and nearly falling over the piano stool.

"Did I startle you?" George Fowler rose from a couch near the windows.

"Oh!" I said again. "I—I didn't see you." Self-consciously, I clapped a hand over my nose.

"Why did 'they' laugh? And who are 'they?'" he inquired.

"Oh, uh—a couple of the servants," I said.

"Really?" He frowned. "Describe them. They're not paid to laugh at guests."

"Oh," I said a fourth time, "they couldn't help it, and if you please, I'd rather not describe them. I don't want to get anyone in trouble. You see, my nose is blue."

"Your nose is blue?" he repeated, amusement gleaming in his eyes. "That could mean one of two things—either that you are blue-blooded or chilly. I am sure it must be the former."

"It's neither." I giggled. "It's ink." I took my hand away. "See?"

He came closer to me. "It does not mar the picture in the least, but if it distresses you . . . " Reaching into his pocket, he brought out a handkerchief.

I had to laugh. "But I can't always be taking your hankerchief," I protested.

"My dear lady," he made me a mock bow, "as my mother has probably already mentioned, our home is at your disposal, which means everything in it—including the handkerchief of your humble servant." Flourishing it, he handed it to me with a second bow.

"Thank you, kind sir," I curtseyed and took it from him, moistening it and rubbing my nose.

"How did you get ink on your nose?"

"Writing in my journal, I expect. I must have touched it. See I've ink on my fingers, too."

"You keep a diary?" He cocked an eyebrow at me. "That's one book I should like to read."

I felt my cheeks burn. "It—it's not very interesting," I murmured, wondering what he would have thought had he seen the morning's entry with its detailed account of his own sad story.

"I should think," he said, moving even closer to me, "that it would be very interesting."

I turned back to the mirror. "There . . . " I said. "It's mostly gone. Thank you for the use of your handkerchief." I put it down on the piano and he took it, returning it to his pocket.

"I shall frame this," he said. "The handkerchief used by Leila MacKenzie, the great prima donna."

"Oh, don't!" I cried.

"Why—what's the matter?" he demanded.

For some reason, his words had brought back all my earlier frustrations. Moving away from him, I said bitterly, "I'm not a great prima donna nor ever likely to be!"

"I can't believe that!" he exclaimed. "I heard you sing. You couldn't have lost that beautiful voice between Sunday and Tuesday."

"Not my v-voice . . . my . . . my p-place," I said. "They're going on to—to San Francisco in—the—the spring without *me*—and it—it's all my fault." I had not meant to cry. I truly had not meant to—but I could not stop myself. Hiding my face in my hands, I wept bitterly.

"Miss MacKenzie." Putting an arm around me, he led me to the couch and pushed me down gently, sitting beside me. "Don't, please." Producing his handkerchief again, he said, "I see I must relinquish this treasured relic." He pressed it against my streaming eyes. "No, I shan't give it to you—I shall hold it the dearer because your tears have dampened it. Did you know that in ancient Rome, they used to catch the Emperor's tears in crystal vases? They were, I believe, considered either magical or medicinal. I wish I had such a container now, for your tears must be musical."

I smiled tremulously. "You—you're being ridiculous."

"So are you, if you say you'll never sing again with that company. They couldn't let such a valuable artist go. Surely when your companion is better, you'll rejoin them?"

"N-no." I shook my head. "C-C-Carlo said . . . he s-s-said . . . "

"What did he say?" George Fowler asked gently.

I had not meant to tell him, but again I could not stop myself. I told him everything that had happened, not sparing myself—the only thing I did not mention was my feeling for Carlo. Drearily, I concluded, "So now you know."

"Now I know that Mr. Carlo or whatever his name is—is both unfeeling and unjust!" he exclaimed.

I regarded him with amazement. "But . . . "

"How could he expect you not to be disappointed?

How could he imagine you would not want to continue singing? Eighteen is not eighty! No, Miss MacKenzie, he was entirely too arbitrary."

Conversely, I felt compelled to defend Carlo, "But he's—he's right, you know. I was being selfish and Lina has been so g-good to me and . . ."

"That is enough. I shall not hear another word on the subject," he said firmly. "Furthermore, nothing you could say would change my opinion of you in the slightest. Would you like to hear what I think about the selfish Leila MacKenzie?"

"I—I . . ."

"Good, I thought you would, and I shall tell you. I think she is delightful—in character, in appearance, and in voice."

"You are very kind," I murmured, feeling terribly foolish. "I don't know why I told you all this. . . ."

"I am glad you did," he said softly. "I am glad of anything that helps me to know you better. Could you guess why I am in here?"

"No."

"Because it was raining and I thought you might come to practice—and you see, I've been rewarded for my vigilance."

I looked away quickly—the intensity of his gaze was unsettling me. I was sure my heart was beating faster. "It—it wasn't much of a reward, with me being so childish as to—to . . ."

"I do not call your grief childish, Miss MacKenzie. Singing obviously means a great deal to you. I wish I had something that meant as much to me."

"But you have all . . ."

"All this?" He grimaced. "This—Sore Thumb? This blot on the golden California landscape? If I had my way, I would have it torn down stick by stick and thrown into the Sacramento River, and all its lands with it. I would pretend it had never existed, for what has it brought any of us except misery? The Bible says that some houses are afflicted with leprosy—this is such a house." He stared into the rain. "How my late and unlamented grandfather must be laughing!"

"L-laughing?" I questioned, a little frightened by his violence.

"Laughing, chortling, snickering, howling with unholy glee." George Fowler bit off each word viciously. "He never wanted any of us to be happy. I suppose you've heard how he died. You couldn't have escaped that story, not with Mrs. Parks around, and I'd imagine she's told you the others as well."

I could not meet his eyes. I said, "She—told me your grandfather died of an apoplectic stroke—that he couldn't speak for years."

"Is that all?" He gave a short bark of a laugh. "She's not quite as well-informed as I imagined. She doesn't know that just before he died, he regained the use of his—forked tongue and spewed out more venom on his sorrowing relatives. Shall I tell you what he said?" Without waiting for my answer, he continued in a sarcastic tone, "He said—'Damn and blast the lot of you, and may you join me in Hell!'"

"Oh," I shivered. "He must have been mad."

"Not mad, my dear, angry—or rather furious that he'd been bilked of the power to spoil our lives as he'd spoiled the lives of his wife, his daughter, and his son. But he succeeded after all for none of us have been happy. We . . . " He broke off abruptly. "You don't want to hear this maudlin blather!"

"Oh, but I do!" I cried. "And it's not maudlin and —and you shouldn't think that just because you had those two unfortunate . . . " I broke off with a gasp. "I—uh . . . "

"You mean Millie and Virginia!" he said with a bitter smile. "I knew she told you. In a way, I'm glad she did."

"She uh—didn't tell me very much . . . " I faltered.

"Come, my dear," he said gently. "You don't need to protect her. All of us are very fond of Mrs. Parks. She's a good sort for all that wagging tongue. She's only concerned for us. At least she doesn't think *I* strangled Virginia and put the blame on Jacinto Morales."

"No one could think that!" I cried.

"You'd be surprised what rumors have spread through this county. Jacinto, you see, was well-liked, a pleasant lad . . . " A brooding expression clouded his eyes. "It seemed incredible to all of us that he killed her. I think it was even incredible to Jacinto. He couldn't explain his motives—not even to the priest who heard his confession at the end."

"They hanged him?"

He nodded. "Yes, I saw it."

"Ugh," I shivered. "Why?"

"I hoped he'd break his silence at the last, but he never did. He went to his execution looking like a martyred Christus, and I, watching, felt like Pontius Pilate."

"Why?" I demanded. "If—he did it . . . "

"Oh, he did it. A gardener heard her screaming. By the time he got there—to the summer house—Jacinto was running out. But still I had a feeling . . . I can't explain it. It doesn't matter, does it? He's dead, and so is she."

"It was a terrible tragedy," I whispered. "You must have loved her very much."

He gave me a long look. "Yes, I did. She was 'a heart whose love is innocent.'"

"Oh," I breathed. "I know that quotation—it's from Byron. 'She walks in Beauty . . . '"

The sadness in his eyes intensified. "Yes, Byron. She used to say . . . " He broke off, flushing. "It doesn't matter."

"She said you look like Byron and you do!" I exclaimed. "I thought so directly I saw you in the station!"

"In the station?" he questioned.

"I mean . . . " I pushed my tongue against my teeth —I was using it too much that morning!

"What did you mean?" he pursued.

There was nothing for me to do but free my tongue

and explain. I did it falteringly, omitting, however, Kezia's remarks about our "motley crew."

"You saw me and I saw you." He nodded.

"You never did!" I exclaimed. "You didn't even look my way. I mean . . . I . . ."

"I did see you," he interrupted, "because when you came on stage in *Traviata*, I recognized you immediately. I said as much to Mother and Kezia. I said, 'I've seen that girl before, but where?' Do you imagine that anyone seeing that lovely little face could ever forget it?"

"Oh, you . . . you shouldn't . . ." I rose from the couch.

He followed me. "Why?" he demanded. "Surely you know you're beautiful. Am I not supposed to know it, too? It's not a secret you can hide."

Fortunately for my peace of mind, I was spared the necessity of answering, for there was a tap on the door and Kezia Graves called, "George, are you in there?" Before he could reply, she entered. "You've got to come right away," she said urgently. "We've had a telephone call from Ethan, and Aunt Aurelia's frantic!"

"From Ethan?" he repeated incredulously. "She hasn't . . ."

Kezia gave him a sharp quelling glance. "We'd best discuss it with Aunt Aurelia," she said crisply, stepping back into the hall. "Are you coming?"

"Of course, right away!" He gave me an apologetic look. "I hope you'll excuse me."

"Please," I murmured, but found myself addressing a closing door.

I had a moment of wondering who Ethan might be. Certainly it was not a woman's name, yet George had said "she." Well, I had heard of women named Lesley and Jo, and there had even been a George Eliot, though of course that had been a woman using a man's name— her real name had been Mary Anne Evans and . . . I realized I was consciously trying to evade the subject uppermost in my mind: George Fowler, whose compliments yet rang in my ears and whose face was more vivid to me than any of my surroundings. Try as I did, I could not deny I was attracted to him—this handsome young man who had suffered so much, so needlessly. In addition to Virginia Soames, there had been Millie Fairchild. How dreadful he must have felt watching me—*her*—come down the aisle and . . . I could not follow the thought to its conclusion. I had to retrace my mental steps to that slip of the mind. I needed no mirror to show me I was blushing a fiery red, for the bride I had envisioned was not Millie Fairchild. She had my face!

I did not see George Fowler any more that day. He did not join us at dinner, and though his mother and Miss Graves were present, the latter was silent and preoccupied. While Mrs. Fowler spoke to me, I had the feeling she did it only out of politeness, for she hardly heeded my answers and her look was abstracted. I was glad when I could return to Lina.

The rest of the day passed quietly. I found a novel in the library and read it to Lina; in the late afternoon, after my nap, I practiced in the music room. I went to bed early.

It rained on Wednesday and Thursday, too. From Mrs. Parks, we learned that the streets of Sacramento were indeed flooded, navigable only by rowboats, canoes, and sailboats. Naturally, no one went to the theater or the opera. Nearly all work was at a standstill, which distressed Lina considerably. I, too, was distressed—not so much on Carlo's account but because that same rain which kept them from performing, kept me in the house, and though I could practice or read, there was not much else to do. Since that morning in the music room, I had not seen George Fowler, and both his mother and cousin were still oddly nervous and upset. I had hoped I might receive some enlightenment from Mrs. Parks, but beyond the fact that George had left the house in the middle of "all that terrible rain on Tuesday afternoon an' hadn't been back since,"

I learned nothing. She had never heard of a woman named "Ethan."

On Friday morning, I awakened early and found that the rain was no longer trickling down my windowpanes. I looked out, hoping to see a cloudless sky, but it was still heavily overcast, and even as I watched, a sinister splatter of drops heralded another downpour. I looked at it in despair—I had never known the heavens could contain so much moisture!

That day bid fair to be like any other day, but in the middle of the morning, Dr. Adams arrived to see Lina. I must say that my hopes rose absurdly when he came out of her room, smiling; they fell as quickly when I remembered that even if she had improved enough to travel, we had nowhere to go except back to Denver!

As it happened, she was better, but Dr. Adams still advised bedrest and no exertion. He had nothing else to tell me, but promised he would know more in another week. I accompanied him downstairs, where he gave much the same report to Mrs. Fowler.

She hardly seemed to be listening, but when he had concluded, she said as before, "She is welcome here. We've plenty of room, and she may stay as long as she wants." She gave me a brief but pleasant smile and, turning back to Dr. Adams, said urgently, "Would you come with me to the back parlor, please? There's something I must ask you."

My heart was heavy as I went upstairs. It seemed to me that the pervading gloom of the storm had also wrought on the inhabitants of the house—certainly something was amiss, and in common with the rain, it appeared to be of a permanent nature. On reaching the head of the stairs, Miss Graves appeared so suddenly that I jumped. I was almost equally startled by her expression. She was smiling!

"Did I alarm you?" she inquired. "I am sorry, but I glimpsed you from down the hall and I did want to speak to you. Have you a minute?"

A minute! Someone had once told me that there are

A Shadow on the House

1224 minutes in a day—I had them all! "Yes," I said, trying not to sigh, "I do."

"Good." She gave me another smile and further astonished me by saying, "It must be very dull for you, here—all this dreadful rain and nothing to do. It's not a very happy situation for an active young girl, especially since your life must have been so full before your friend's unfortunate illness."

Inwardly I winced. Was she deliberately taunting me? I searched her face for corroboration of my suspicions but found none; she still continued to smile at me and her eyes were actually benign! I said, "Oh, no I don't find it dull here—it's very pleasant and you've all been so . . . " I paused. My tongue had balked at the word "kind." It was beginning to sound banal. "Besides," I finished lamely, "I have my music."

"But that's hardly enough to keep you occupied all day, and since you can't go outdoors, I wondered if you mightn't like to see the rest of this house. It's quite interesting, you know, and I'd be delighted to give you an informal guided tour."

Amazement momentarily robbed me of speech, but finally I managed to say, "That would be lovely! I should very much like to see more of this house."

"Good. Shall we do it now?"

"Oh, yes, please, Miss Graves," I said eagerly. I almost clapped my hands.

"You mustn't call me 'Miss Graves,'" she admonished. "My name is Kezia."

"Very well, Kezia," I said. "Mine is Leila."

"A charming name. Leila MacKenzie—it has a certain ring to it. I am sure you will make it famous."

"I hope so," I said. Her gracious manner was beginning to have its effect on me. Though I could not imagine what had caused the change in her attitude, I felt she was being sincere.

I was sure of it when she said, "I know you will. I've heard you practicing. I am delighted that I'll have the chance to listen to you for yet another week. I hope you don't mind that I have sometimes—listened?" She actually looked anxious.

"Not at all!" I exclaimed.

"Good. I'm glad you know about my eavesdropping. I abhor the clandestine!"

"An audience should never be clandestine!" I laughed. "Please come in the next time."

"I certainly shall, and thank you. Now, we can either start up here, or downstairs. Which would you prefer?"

"Since we're here, let's start here," I said.

"Fine. Now on this floor there are fifteen rooms, some single, some suites. The singles are generally for guests—my aunt, my cousin, and I all have suites. I may not show you those, but since they're much like the one you occupy, I am sure you have an idea about them. I think we'll start here." Moving down the hall, she opened a door to an octagonal chamber with painted walls divided by pink marble frames; the ceiling was concave and of sculptured plaster centered by a Venetian glass chandelier. The canopied bed was covered by a delicate pink spread and there was a mirrored dressing table draped in pink ruffled silk. A small pink marble mantelpiece was adorned by a variety of delicate china figures, including a clock made of twining china flowers, topped by a cupid holding aloft a golden goblet. "Oh," I breathed. "How charming."

She shrugged. "I find it a bit too ornate for my taste. My aunt was inspired by a similar room she discovered in a French chateau. Then, too, I think there's too much china. I never cared much for Dresden. It breaks too easily." I wondered if she were remembering some childhood incident—broken china in a disordered room where a man had beaten his wife to death? I wished I did not know her history; it seemed like eavesdropping, somehow, but I knew I would never have enough courage to tell her I had "listened." I was glad when we left the little room.

We went into several other guest-chambers, all of which were beautifully furnished—in fact, there were so many glowing carpets, crystal chandeliers, inlaid tables, expensive knickknacks, that I was actually becoming sated by the lavishness of my surroundings. "There's so much!" I exclaimed, as we emerged from another room. "Your aunt did all the decorating?"

"Nearly all," Kezia replied. "She worked very hard."

"She must have!" I exclaimed. Then, thinking I had better be more appreciative, I continued, "It's very well planned."

"I shall tell her you said so. It will please her. She would have taken you around, herself, but as I am sure you've noticed, she is sadly preoccupied these days."

"I have noticed," I said. "I hope nothing is wrong."

Kezia's eyes rested on mine for a moment. Her expression was enigmatic and so were her words. "Nothing that cannot be mended in time and with patience." Turning down another corridor, she said, "We've come into the Norman wing, now, and here is my grandfather's bedroom. You'll not find any of my aunt's handiwork here—it was of his designing, and since his death it has remained undisturbed." She opened a door on our right; it swung back with a loud squeak. "Undisturbed and unoiled!" she exclaimed sharply. "Servants always neglect this wing."

We came into a large square chamber with a high ceiling and small slits of windows set in deep alcoves. With the exception of the bed, which was very large, with an ornately carved wooden headboard and footboard, it was furnished in almost monastic simplicity. There were no pictures, but near the door hung a large mirror in a silver frame. There was a musty, damp odor about the place that made me cough.

"I hope you're not getting a cold!" Kezia said.

"No." I noticed a large Bible on the dresser. "Was your grandfather a religious man?" I asked.

She smiled wryly. "Not when he was younger, but in his long illness, it was hoped that the Bible might bring him comfort. No one knows if it did, for he could not speak." She had moved to the head of the bed and now she faced me, her eyes fixed on mine. "Just think, Leila," she said in a low voice. "No one knew what he was thinking. He'd had a stroke, you see, and for twelve years he lay on this bed, silently, without moving. Only his eyes moved. He would watch people as they entered his room—he could see them in that mirror behind you, see them come down the hall and enter his room, walking across this floor. He watched their every gesture; nothing escaped those black eyes of his—back and forth they moved, back and forth, watching, watching, watching."

She was toying with a little watch she wore around her neck; absently she swung it between her fingers. "Watching, as they moved back and forth," she continued. "Otherwise, he was useless—his hands and feet were like dry withered twigs; his whole body like a motionless log, a mighty, fallen treetrunk, Leila. He was dependent on the kindness of hired servants, who hated him for what he had been when he was well— but then, servants are never your friends. No one is your friend who depends on you financially. They are always resentful. Any one of them, moving back and forth in this room, was stronger than he. How he must have resented that! And perhaps he feared them, too, for they could easily have ended his life by strangling or smothering him—but they let him live because they knew living was the worst punishment. They let him live until he died from natural causes."

I had been listening with some impatience, having already heard the story of old George Fowler from Mrs. Parks and his grandson—both of whom had told it in a briefer and more interesting form. Kezia's monotonous manner of speaking had nearly put me to sleep. However, when she had reached what I hoped was the end of her narrative, I said, "Gracious, you made me feel as if he were actually here in this room, lying on the bed." I achieved an artistic shudder. "Brrrr. Poor man."

Much to my surprise, her eyes gleamed with anger. "Yes," she snapped, "he suffered for his sins." She went to the door. The other rooms in this wing are of scant interest—they are used mainly for storage. There's a lovely view from the top of this tower, but since the weather precludes our enjoying it, would you like to go downstairs?"

"Very much," I tried to sound enthusiastic, but I was thinking that I had had enough of the tour, and even though Kezia had been friendly, I still did not feel quite comfortable with her.

Perhaps she was equally ill-at-ease with me, for when we had returned to the stairs, she glanced at her watch and said crisply, "I must go. There are things I have to do. If you choose, you can continue the tour alone."

If I was surprised by her abrupt dismissal, I was also delighted. "I shouldn't mind at all."

"Good." She hurried away so quickly that I decided that she must have been as eager as I to end her self-imposed duty.

I did not go downstairs; instead, I returned to my room and inscribed the encounter in my journal. Later, reading what I had written, I was puzzled by the incident. Why had she proposed the tour? Out of the kindness of her heart? I doubted it. Though I did not know her well, I was positive that kindness was not one of her predominant virtues. Furthermore, I did not believe she wanted to be friends with me—there had been nothing friendly about her after we had left her grandfather's room. Thinking back on it, it had been just about then that her attitude had become, once more, cold and condescending. Perhaps the thought of her grandfather's suffering had depressed her? I could hardly believe that. Her description of his last years had been devoid of sympathy—devoid, indeed, of all human feeling. In fact, I could not imagine why she had chosen to talk about him. Truly, she had some odd, puzzling ways. As I closed my book, I hoped that I might be spared any more overtures of friendship from Kezia Graves.

When I arose from my siesta that afternoon, I found that the rain had stopped. The sky was a cloud-dappled blue and the foliage gleamed yellow-green in the fading sunlight. My spirits lifted. I do not think I have ever appreciated the combined beauties of earth and sky as I did that afternoon. Though the ground was soaking wet, I was as eager to set foot on it as Noah from his ark, but unlike that venerable patriarch, I had to consider my throat. I did not want to risk a cold, and so I stayed in my room. In my journal, I wrote, "Let the night come quickly and the morning soon." To my mind, it sounded very poetical, and thinking of poetry, a tiny vision of George Fowler appeared at the back of my eyes. I wondered where he had gone—more pertinently, I wondered when he would be coming back.

Though the grounds were still damp and the trees were dripping water, Saturday's sun was high, hot, and bright and I was determined to go outside. I did not discuss my plan with Lina, because I knew she would protest. I knew I was risking a chill, but I was a little defiant, because if it had been able to follow its schedule, the Benedetto Opera Troupe would be on its way to Stockton. It was an embittering thought, and equally embittering was the realization that the train taking it away from Sacramento also bore Carlo Benedetto out of my life. Quite possibly, I would never see him again.

"It does not matter." I wrote in the journal that was beginning to be my greatest confidant. "IT DOES NOT MATTER!!!" But even though I put it in capitals and underlined it three times with a ferocity that split my penpoint, I knew it did matter. I knew, too, that tears were not far away; but I would not cry. Arming myself with my parasol, I hurried down the stairs and in a few moments had stepped into the garden.

I might have gone anywhere had I been master or rather mistress of my feet, but as it happened, I could not keep them from walking in the direction of the Shakespearean garden. I did not really want to go—I was positive of that—but I could not stop myself. As iron filings toward a steel magnet, I was drawn toward that cedar hedge, that rustic gate. Yielding to the inevitable, I went inside.

A Shadow on the House

It was even more beautiful than I remembered. The flowers and trees were brighter; the rain-washed statuary was a pristine white against the clean blue sky, and there was the oak Carlo had climbed. It was all too easy for me to visualize him sitting among the branches, his dark hair tousled, his brown eyes laughing into mine. It was, of course, entirely foolish to run through those damp grasses and embrace that tree, but I did. There were other steps to retrace, down the slope to the willow-bordered pond. The stream was now more turbulent, swollen by the rains and almost overlapping its banks. I could not see Ophelia's arm. I really did not want to see it, but . . . I tensed; I had heard something. It sounded like weeping. Looking around me, I saw nothing, but the sobbing continued. It seemed to be all around me. I had the strange fancy that Ophelia herself had returned to haunt the gardens, but since she was a fictional character and since statues do not weep, I decided to probe further into the matter.

Moving in what I imagined was the direction of the sound, I said tentatively, "Who are you? Where are you? What is the matter?"

I received no answer. Someone did whistle, but that was a distance away—probably one of the gardeners, working in the rosebeds beyond the hedge.

"I—I did not mean to do it . . . " It was a girl's voice. Where was it coming from?

The bushes perhaps? I drew nearer and saw something white behind a tall fern. Cautiously, I parted two of its fronds and peered down—at a crouching woman! To this day, I do not know how I managed to quell the scream that rose to my lips, for certainly, the creature before me seemed more like an apparition than a living being. Painfully thin, she was clad in a gown so badly torn that it barely sufficed to cover her nakedness. There was a filthy rag tied about her straggling yellow hair, and what little I could see of her face was streaked with grime. Her feet were bare, the soles cracked and bloodied, as if she had walked a long way. She had not ceased to weep, and intermingled with her sobbing were disjointed phrases that were mostly unintelligible.

My first impulse was to summon help, but as I hesitated, she looked up at me. Suprise immobilized me. I had not known what to expect, but I had not anticipated that she would be so young. Yes, even though there were great hollows under her eyes, even though her features were emaciated, she could not have been more than twenty-two. It was also possible to see that she had once been lovely—the eyes that were fixed on mine were bloodshot, but they were also a vivid violet. She had stopped crying and her unwavering stare was frightening in its intensity. I knew I ought to run for help, but her proximity to the stream gave me pause. I could now see the glimmer of that sunken statue. Who knew what message it might communicate to a girl obviously as mad as Ophelia?

Very gently, I said, "Can I help you?"

Her gaze had shifted; she was looking behind me. In a stricken whisper, she said, "I did not mean to do it. . . . I don't know why I did, George. You know I love you. Why would I run away from you—when with all my being, I longed to—to be possessed by you? From the first moment I saw you, I loved you. I—I've never loved anyone else. Won't you forgive me? See . . . " She smoothed her ragged gown. "I've put on my wedding dress . . . . Oh, I was so afraid it would not be finished in time. . . . " Rising, she touched the cloth around her head. "And this is my grandmother's veil. . . . Something old . . . something new . . . something borrowed . . . something blue . . . " Her giggle, high and eerie, made me shiver. "You'd never guess what the blue is. . . . You won't see it until we're together . . . upstairs in our bridal chamber. Am I being indelicate, George? But you know I love you . . . and when two people are in love . . . a wife must cleave unto her husband. . . . That's the Bible . . . " She cocked her head. . . . "Oh, it's starting . . . the wedding march . . . I'm ready . . . " She took a step toward me.

I moved around the fern to face her. "Please . . . "

A SHADOW ON THE HOUSE 147

I put out my hand. "Don't . . . " I stopped talking. One could not reason with that poor demented girl. How had she happened to come to this garden? What strange set of circumstances had drawn her so near the statue of mad Ophelia? Was it a coincidence, or had she—Millie Fairchild—strolled through this same garden in happier days, looked into the water, seen the statue, and somehow remembered it? She had taken another step in my direction. Instinctively, I backed away from her. But she did not even look at me; her eyes were still fixed on a point behind me and she seemed to be holding the arm of someone. Her father? I said, "Millie, please . . . " She paid no heed to me. She was listening to another sound—the wedding march.

I did not know what to do! I was really afraid to leave the poor girl to her own mad devices. Then I remembered the whistling I had heard—that gardener could not be far away. I could fetch him. It would take only a few minutes at the most, but what if he were not there?

While I deliberated, Millie Fairchild abruptly veered away from me and ran toward the water's edge. In almost a normal voice she said, "I came here to do something. Oh, yes, I remember. I do remember!" Deliberately, she threw herself into the water.

"No!" I screamed. "No, you mustn't!" Flinging myself down on the bank, I grabbed at her dress. The ragged material parted under my frenzied clutch. "Please . . . please . . ." I begged. "Millie, come back . . . come back . . . " I could not make her listen. She had moved into deeper water. It was reaching her chin. Rising, I made another futile grab for her and, overbalancing, fell into the stream. Beneath me, I felt the hard but slippery ridges of the statue. I could not obtain a foothold. I plunged forward, grabbing Millie; then, to my horror, she wrapped her arms around me and started to pull me down. She was strong—unusually strong. For a moment, I could not loosen her grasp. Then, behind me, I saw the arm of the statue and managed to grasp it. It, too, was slippery beneath my fingers, but still I obtained a hold on it, while behind me the girl continued to pull at me. My heavy skirts, weighted by the water, were another hazard. I screamed and screamed again—then I heard a man's voice call.

"Where are you, for Gawd's sake?"

"Shakespeare!" I yelled back. "Help us . . . help me . . . " My hands were slipping. I could not hold on much longer, not with frenzied Millie Fairchild clutching at me. Her eyes were rolling wildly, and the sounds she was making had long ceased to resemble anything human.

As I struggled to evade her, my panic increased, for the water was very cold, my limbs were growing numb, and my fingers were losing their feeling. Soon I should be unable to hang onto that marble arm—soon I should be dragged under the water to die, as Ophelia had died! Hoarsely, I screamed, "Help . . . hurry . . . hurry . . . help . . . " Then above me, I heard the blessed, blessed words.

"Lord love-a-duck, wot'n 'ell's this?"

Two men had leaped down to the water's edge, and a moment later, they had dragged us from the pond. Mercifully, Millie Fairchild fainted. I did not. I could even answer the questions of my astounded rescuers. "She . . . drowned . . . wanted to drown herself, I mean . . . I wanted to help her . . . but I fell in. . . . " I did not have the strength to walk back to the house—I had to let them carry me.

Mrs. Fowler met us in the hall. She was shaking her head and actually wringing her hands. "God . . . a terrible thing . . . You might've been killed, girlie. Take her up to her room. Wait! Kezia, get the brandy!"

"Yes, at once." Kezia hurried down the corridor. She was back in a moment with a cut-glass decanter, which Mrs. Fowler took and held to my lips.

"Take a big swallow!" she advised. "Go on—a big one."

On obeying, I coughed and spluttered as the fiery liquid went down. "Oh . . . "

"Another swallow!" she ordered.

A Shadow on the House

I could not protest, not with the bottle at my lips. I obeyed again. It was warming, but when I was taken to my room, I was very dizzy. It is only vaguely that I remember Lina leaning on Mrs. Parks's arm and looking at me with pity and concern. I think I mumbled that I was all right. I think she kissed me. I also remember seeing Dr. Adams and George. I recall being surprised at seeing George and muttering, "You're back," and something about poor Millie, but I was hardly aware of anything much until midafternoon, when I awakened to find myself in bed, wearing a warm, voluminous nightdress and under heaps of blankets.

At first I lay there, rejoicing in the fact that I was alive and dry. Then I grew cold with fright as I recalled my experience in more detail. I had been wet, I had screamed—not once but often—and what had that done to my voice, my precious, precious voice? Was it still there? I had to know! Sitting upright in bed, I drew a long tremulous breath and sang what I hoped would be a high C. Much to my relief, it came out loud and clear.

It was followed by a hoarse cry. Into my field of vision popped Mrs. Fowler, while from the adjoining room Mrs. Parks hurried in. Both women gaped at me in horror.

"She's delirious!" Mrs. Fowler exclaimed.

"Has to be!" Mrs. Parks agreed. "That was an awful-soundin' shriek!"

"Awful-sounding shriek!" I echoed indignantly. "It was a high C!"

"That's right." Lina had followed Mrs. Parks and now she moved to the end of my bed and sat down. "It was right on pitch, too. You don't need to worry, my darling. The voice is unharmed." She frowned. "But you were a very foolish girl to take such a risk."

"She was a very brave girl!" Mrs. Fowler exclaimed warmly. "I wish I had me a daughter like her." She gave me a hug. "I've got to get George," she said. "I told him I'd let him know the minute you waked up." She hurried out of the room.

"Oh, dear!" I exclaimed. "I never asked her about Millie Fairchild. It was Millie Fairchild, wasn't it?"

"Sure was," Mrs. Parks said, "an' the whole police force from Sacramento and two neighborin' counties lookin' for her!"

"But what happened to her?" I demanded. "Is she all right?"

"Poor, poor girl." Lina sighed.

"She didn't . . . she wasn't drowned? She'd only fainted, I thought," I said falteringly.

"Yes, honey, now don't get all upset," Mrs. Parks cautioned. "She's all right—right as she'll ever be, considerin' she's plumb crazy. Lord, there's no tellin' how she got here, with half the county on the lookout for her, an' dogs an' everythin'! She's been gone since Tuesday!"

"Tuesday!" I exclaimed. "Is—is that why Mrs. Fowler's been so disturbed, and George . . ."

"Yeah," Mrs. Parks answered. "Seems her pa called here on Tuesday—wanted him to come an' help hunt for her. They didn't think she'd gone very far—thought the sight of George might help restore her wits."

"She must've seen him this morning. Did it help her?" I asked.

"Nope, didn't know him. Didn't know nobody. They come an' took her away in a straitjacket, poor thing. Crazy as a coot."

I shuddered. "Oh, dear, she must have loved him so much!"

"Then why'd she hightail it for the hinterlands that day?" Mrs. Parks demanded. "Nobody made her do it. It was her own idea."

I thought of Millie's words that morning. "Maybe it was a moment of panic. It's too bad he wouldn't give her a chance to explain."

"Humph!" Mrs. Parks shrugged. "What was there to explain? Must've been crazy even then. To my way of thinkin' he's well rid of her."

"Oh, don't," I protested. "If you—you'd seen her this morning . . ." Tears stung my eyelids. "It—it was dreadful. Poor, poor girl . . . . If only I could've made her understand . . . "

"Don't take it so much to heart, my darling," Lina murmured. "Mrs. Parks is probably right. She must have been mentally unsound from the very beginning." She smoothed my hair back gently. "You know, my dear, I'm very proud of you. I think I've underestimated you in many ways . . . . You're a very courageous girl. You . . . " She paused, gasping for breath. "You . . . "

"Lina!" I exclaimed. "You've got to go back to bed!"

"That's right!" Mrs. Parks hurried to her side. "What'm I doin' lettin' you stand 'round here an' shoot the breeze. You come with me . . . "

"But . . . " she began.

"Please, Lina," I urged. "Go with her. You shouldn't be up."

After she and Mrs. Parks had gone into the other room, I began to cry in earnest, though I could not have said whether it was because of Millie's plight, Lina's illness or the reaction from my exertions of the morning. Then, of course, there was that Stockton-bound train, but I would not think of that—I was *not* crying for Carlo. Angrily, I wiped my eyes. Crying solved nothing! I thought of Millie again—of those hollowed, bloodshot eyes. How many useless tears had fallen from them? Imagine loving someone that much! If that was how real love affected you, then what Lina had once said to me was true—I did not really love Carlo. It was only that he—that I—. Before I could sort out my jumbled thoughts, there was a tap on my door.

"Yes?" I called.

"May I come in?" George asked, opening the door a crack.

"Please," I said.

He strode over to my bed. "Thank God, you're safe!" he said emotionally. "Why did you try to save her yourself? Why didn't you go for help? Any one of the gardeners would have come!"

"I was afraid of what might happen to her—she was so distraught."

"God!" he exclaimed. "When I think what might have happened to you!" Pulling up a chair, he sat by me. "You were within inches of drowning!"

"But I didn't drown," I said reasonably.

He barely heeded me. "Such a shattering experience for you—that poor demented creature. We've been searching for her for days, and all the while she was here!"

His detached manner of speaking about her disturbed me. "That poor demented creature, as you call her, loved you dreadfully," I said coldly.

He shook his head. "I think not," he said crisply. "You did not know her before her illness. She was the spoiled only daughter of a very wealthy man, and though I was not aware of it at the time, she was full of whims and caprices. That's why she deserted me at the altar. Then, after dealing me what was tantamount to a mortal blow, she expected I would take her back as if nothing had happened. I, however, am not her indulgent father." He had spoken with a deep bitterness which I could understand. Undoubtedly, he had received a dreadful shock, but still I could not help being almost equally sorry for poor little Millie Fairchild.

George Fowler did not stay with me very long, which was well for my peace of mind because while he remained, he insisted on holding my hand—a favor I should not have granted, but I told myself I was too weak to plead proprieties. I was also too weak to protest the kiss he pressed upon my forehead when he left. However, I resolved that once I recovered, I would be cool, distant, and ladylike. Really, his resemblance to Byron was very marked—but what did that have to do with anything? In self-defense, I prepared to sleep again, and rendered defenseless by sleep, I dreamed of George in a garden. Millie Fairchild was not there.

I spent most of Sunday in bed, venturing only as far as Lina's room; though I had not caught a cold, I had all manner of aches and pains, as well as several bruises on my legs and feet. The morning passed pleasantly enough—I read, I wrote in my journal, and I dozed. That afternoon, George and his mother came to visit me, but Kezia did not cement our newly formed friendship by accompanying them. When I asked after her, Mrs. Fowler looked concerned. "She's got a sick headache. She's been driven nearly distracted by what happened to poor Millie."

"You'd better tell her the rest, Mother," George said meaningfully. "Just in case . . ."

Mrs. Fowler regarded him anxiously. "I hope it don't happen a second night."

"But if it does, she'd better know. In fact, maybe Leila'd better lock her door."

"Maybe she ought," Mrs. Fowler agreed. "I wouldn't want her being scared out of half her natural growth."

I could have told her that I was already beginning to be alarmed by the puzzling ambiguity of their conversation. "Why would I be scared?" I could not refrain from asking.

"Well, you see," Mrs. Fowler said hesitantly, "Kezia walked last night."

"In her sleep," George clarified. "She hasn't done it for a long time."

"Hardly at all since she was a litle girl," Mrs. Fowler corroborated, with a wry, half-smile. "Last night, though, she walked the length of the corridor—dead asleep. Frightened Mary half to death. Thought she was a ghost."

"It's a good thing Mary didn't rouse her," George commented.

"Good thing is right," his mother said. "Might've waked the whole house with her yelling, which wouldn't have been very good for the morale of the servants." She looked at me. "Anyhow, mightn't be a bad idea to lock your door—you never know where she'll go. Could give you a shock if you were to wake and find her there."

"I'll lock it," I said. "She must have been very fond of Millie."

"Yes, she was," Mrs. Fowler replied. "They were great friends. Millie cottoned to her right from the start, and Kezia liked her better than practically anyone she knew. It surprised me at the time—they weren't a bit similar."

It surprised me, too, since I could not imagine Kezia Graves being particularly fond of anyone. However, I contented myself with saying, "Millie must have been a sweet girl, before her illness."

"Sweet as sugar," Mrs. Fowler grimaced. "Bit too sweet for my digestion—not that I ever said as much to George." She looked at him challengingly. "Did I?"

"You never did," he acknowledged. "Maybe you should have."

"I don't believe in that," she stated. "A person has to make his own decisions and his own mistakes."

"Even if it leads to marriage, Mother?"

"As to that, I thought she'd be a good enough wife. She loved you—didn't seem to be any doubt of that." Her eyes grew perplexed. "I couldn't anticipate what'd happen. I still don't understand what got into that fool girl. Day before the wedding, she was as bright and chipper as a cricket. You can ask Kezia—she spent part of the day with her. And then, to fly off like that! Sure beats me why she did it."

"Let's don't talk about it any more, please," George said sharply. Making what I considered an unfortunate allusion, he added, "It's all water under the bridge."

That night, I went to sleep early. Just before I closed my eyes, I remembered I had not locked my door. I was too drowsy to rectify the ommission, but either Kezia did not walk or she took another direction, for my slumbers remained unbroken.

I was rather lethargic on Monday, but by Tuesday, I felt myself again. Dr. Adams, who had come to see Lina, agreed with me. He had other good news for me. "Miss Lina is much better," he declared, smiling at her. "Another week and she should be well enough to travel."

"Do tell!" Mrs. Parks exclaimed. "Only another week?"

"Oh!" Lina's eyes gleamed. "I am glad of that. I've imposed on the Fowlers far too long."

"Yes," I agreed, "far too long." Moving to her bed, I kissed her. "I'm so glad, Lina, so relieved." Out of concern for her, I did not mention what was uppermost in my mind—our return to Denver, because that was undoubtedly where we would go. It was the only place we *could* go, and then—what would happen to me? I could not imagine—or rather, I could imagine all too well—exactly what would happen. Nothing. I would stay and stagnate for years, possibly forever, and ironically enough, precisely at the time Lina and I would be arriving in Denver, the Benedetto Troupe would be in San Francisco . . . . San Francisco in the spring!

"Only another week?" Mrs. Fowler made a swipe at the centerpiece and pushed it down the dining table. "I can't see you," she complained. She frowned at me. "I can't believe your friend'll have improved that much in just seven more days. She'll have to give herself more time."

"Yes," George agreed. "She doesn't look that well to me. I don't care what Adams said."

"Lina feels she has imposed on you long enough," I told them.

"Nonsense," Mrs. Fowler snapped. "I'm going to have a talk with Miss Lina this afternoon—going to tell her we want to keep you both a mite longer. Why, with all this ruckus, I haven't had a chance to get to know you."

"But Aunt Aurelia"—Kezia broke her silence for the first time since we had sat down to dinner—"Leila has her singing. You'll be rejoining your company, won't you?"

"No," George said, "they had to make other arrangements, which is all the more reason why she must stay." He smiled at me, saying firmly, "We insist."

I looked away—as usual, I found his gaze unsettling. I said, "I can't unless Lina agrees, and knowing her, I don't think she will. However, I will always be grateful to all of you for your help. Without you, I don't know what we would have done."

"Oh, come," Mrs. Fowler rasped, "there's no need to start your farewells, now, my dear. Lots can happen in a week!"

"Lots," George agreed, his eyes seeking mine.

I happened to catch sight of my face reflected in a silver salver. Much to my annoyance, I discovered I was blushing.

Shortly after dinner, I went to practice, choosing the theater in preference to the music room. As I entered the building, the sight of its seats, its stage, and its golden curtain brought a return of my depression. When would I sing in a real opera house again? When I was twenty-one and able to call myself an adult? I sighed. Many women were married at my age, and if a woman could be married and could bear children at eighteen or younger, why . . . I groaned. I could convince myself with my arguments, but Lina and Mama were another story.

Sitting down at the piano, I commenced my scales. My voice responded so beautifully that my misery increased. I could *not* go back to Denver! I had to continue with my singing! If I stopped now, I might never be able to start again. "Oh," I wailed, "please God, help me . . . help me . . . " Leaning my head against the piano, I burst into tears.

"Leila!"

Startled, I swung around on the stool to find George hurrying down the aisle. "I—I didn't know," I began. "I—Mr. Fowler—uh—George, you mustn'tttttttt!"

He had taken me in his arms and pressed his lips on mine, effectively silencing my objections. Finally, he released me, and of course, I should have slapped his face, run out of the theater, or at least have drawn myself up to my full height and haughtily denounced him. To have looked at him wonderingly, to have touched his cheek gently, while whispering "Oh, George," was only inviting more of the same disgraceful treatment, which I received immediately and to which I responded in the same inarticulate and highly improper manner. I cannot even say that I closed my eyes and pretended it was Carlo, for when he let me speak, I murmured a second time, "George . . . George!" and committed the final indiscretion of wrapping my arms around his neck and embracing *him!*

Minutes later, we drew apart. My heart was beating very fast, and there were numerous other parts of my anatomy with similar pulsations . . . sensations? I am not sure if I am describing my reactions correctly. It is very difficult to find the words to express my feelings at that time. I seem to recollect that there was also a roaring in my ears. He must have been similarly affected, for he breathed like a man who has just concluded a cross-country race; his face was flushed and his voice husky. "I can't let you go," he said. "No matter what happens, I can't let you go."

"No, you mustn't," I murmured, which again was the wrong response, because now would have been the time to redeem myself with a sobbing, "Oh, dear, I don't know what came over me. What must you think of me?" Unfortunately, the things we ought to say never do occur to us at the proper moment.

He ran a finger down my cheek. "You were crying," he said. "Why were you crying?"

"I don't remember," I said truthfully. At that moment, nothing mattered except the immediate present so entirely occupied by George. I said, "George . . . Lord Byron, he was a George, too. George Gordon Noel . . . in my English literature . . . "

He paled. "No," he cried. "Don't say that, don't." He threw his arms around me and held me tightly, "I'll not lose you, too." His face crumpled. Releasing me, he thrust his fists into his eyes and wept like a child. "I couldn't bear it. Not again . . . not again."

I took his hand. "Darling, darling." It was amazing how quickly the endearments crowded to my lips. "Don't—you won't lose me. You mustn't cry . . . "

"You don't understand," he whispered. "You spoke with Virginia's tongue. The very words—the very w-words she said—when we first . . . " He shook his head.

Virginia Soames. Poor Virginia Soames. The name echoed unpleasantly through my mind and I felt chilled. For a moment, I wanted to run from him, but I could not leave him. "George," I said gently, "I remember now. You told me that she, too, called you that, but I shan't. Not any more. I'll never mention his name again. You mustn't be afraid for me, my dear. Lightning never strikes in the same place twice, they say." Even as I spoke, I recalled that disasters did come in threes, but I forgot it when he pulled me back to him and kissed me yet again.

Finally, I broke from him. "No more," I said breathlessly. "Please we—mustn't anymore." I hurried up the aisle.

He followed me. "Leila," he said, as we came into the sunshine. "Wait, don't leave me yet. There's something I must say to you . . . . Come." He drew me toward the rose garden. In a corner near the wall, there was a little marble bench. "Sit here, please," he begged.

I hesitated. Suddenly I was nervous, though I could not have told him why. I remained standing. "I ought to go inside. I . . . Lina . . . "

"Not yet." He pointed to the bench. "Please sit down."

"Well . . . for a minute," I said, as I complied. To my amazement, he knelt before me.

"Leila," he said in a rush, "will you be my wife?"

"You—you can't be serious!" I exclaimed. "You hardly know me. I mean . . . I mean . . . you hardly do. Oh, please don't keep on kneeling. What would anyone say if they saw you?"

"They'd say that I was kneeling to a goddess—my goddess of love, my beautiful Venus!" he said.

It was utterly reprehensible of me, but I had a wild desire to laugh. It was with considerable difficulty that I subdued it. I couldn't laugh at such a serious moment. I said weakly, "B-b-but, G-George."

He seized my hand. "Are you afraid of me?" he asked huskily.

"Afraid, n-no, but . . ."

He pressed my hand to his lips. "I love you," he said. "I've loved you since the first day I saw you. I didn't think I would ever have the courage to say that to a woman again. I did not think I would ever want to say it again. I thought my heart was dead, but you have brought it back to life again. You have brought me back to life. I was a marble statue—you have made me flesh again!"

I wished that he would not express himself so extravagantly, because again I had to quell a burgeoning smile. "George," I began.

"You love me, too," he interrupted. "You couldn't have responded to me as you did, if you didn't"

Confusion was clouding my perceptions. I *had* enjoyed kissing him. It had been very pleasant. But did that mean I loved him? I could not be sure. I thought of Carlo. Had my sensations been the same that day in the Shakespearean garden? Perhaps if I could have kissed him and then kissed George, I could have decided more easily—as it was, I was not at all sure as to the extent or even the nature of my feelings for George, and I could only wish he was not being so very precipitate.

"George." I paused, wondering what I might tell him. "I . . ."

"Don't say anything now," he ordered. "Think!"

"Think?" I repeated. "Yes." I looked at him gratefully. "That is what I must do. Think."

"But," he said, "don't keep me waiting too long, my darling."

"Oh, I shan't," I promised rashly.

"When might I have your answer, my angel?" he questioned, staring at me intently.

Really, he was so handsome. I had seen pictures of Lord Byron that did not do him justice—at least, I was sure they did not do him justice because they did not compare with the ones that, in my estimation, must look exactly like him because that's the way a man who wrote so beautifully ought to look. But George did the best of his portraits justice. If he had worn a rolled open collar, he . . . Mentally, I paused. Where were my thoughts straying? What had he asked? Oh, yes, he demanded an answer. I suppose, I said to myself, it ought to be yes.

"Yes!" he repeated. "It not only ought to be, it must be." Dropping down on the bench beside me, he slipped his arm around my waist. "It is yes, isn't it, Leila, my own?"

I stared at him in horrified amazement. How had he been able to read my innermost thoughts? Unless I had spoken them aloud, as I sometimes did when alone . . . . Had I? I had! "Oh, I . . ." I started to protest.

"You said 'yes,'" he reminded me. "I shall hold you to it."

"You shall? I mean—you will?" I whispered weakly.

"Forever!" he exclaimed, embracing me again.

It was really so pleasant when he kissed me that I could only respond in kind—and consequently, when at length we went back to the house and parted at the stairs, he said, "I shall tell Mother we are engaged."

Until I had transcribed the events of that afternoon in my journal, it did not occur to me that as George's fiancée, I should not have to go back to Denver! I could . . . That gave me pause. What could I do? Would he want me to go on with my singing? Suppose he didn't. Suppose . . . ?

"Leila!" Lina tapped on the adjoining door. "May I come in?"

"Please," I said, wondering if I ought to tell her.

She entered, smiling and looking much better than she had even that morning. "Oh, I am so glad you're back!" she exclaimed. "I've something to tell you. I've had a letter from Carlo."

"C-Carlo?" I repeated. "A letter?"

She nodded happily, and perching on the end of my bed, she continued, "My dear, you will sing in San Francisco after all!"

My knees went weak. I fell on the bed. "S-San Francisco?"

"Carlo needs you for a *Traviata*. You must report there for rehearsal on April eighteenth."

"B-but he said . . . he said . . . " I could not tell her what he had said to me.

She put her hand on my shoulder. "My dear, I know you had a little quarrel—he mentions it in his letter. He also said for me to tell you that he thinks he was too hard on you. Carlo is quick-tempered, but his angers are never lasting. He has written that he might arrange a chaperon for you if I am not well enough to come. But I am."

"You are! But you couldn't travel all that way, Lina!"

"San Francisco is not as far as Denver. Oh, my dear, I am much improved. Why, darling, what's the matter?"

I had leaped to my feet and was pacing back and forth. "If I'd only known before. But it shouldn't make any difference, should it? It can't. Oh, Lina—shall I really sing in San Francisco in the spring!"

"You really will, but why . . . ?"

I came back to her, and kneeling on the floor beside the bed, I cried, "Oh, Lina, I—I'm engaged!"

"Engaged?" she repeated incredulously. "To whom?"

"To George, of course," I exclaimed.

She listened gravely while I told her what had happened. When I had concluded my account, she said, "Do you love him, then?"

I looked at her mournfully. "I—don't know. I thought . . . Carlo . . . I mean I had thought—Carlo until—and then—George, he's very handsome, Lina, and I liked it when he—when he—he—"

She paled. "When he what?" she demanded.

"Well . . ." I hesitated. "He . . . he . . ."

She grabbed my hands, held them tightly, looked at me fiercely. "Tell me all! What did he do to you?"

"He kissed me rather often, I'm afraid. I know I should've stopped him but . . ." I paused because she was laughing—in my estimation, immoderately loudly. "I don't see anything amusing about it!" I said indignantly.

"It's not amusing, my darling," she assured me quickly. "It's only that I thought . . ." She smiled at me. "It doesn't matter what I thought. Oh, but you are an innocent, though. And didn't I predict you'd forget Carlo soon enough, my dear?"

"But I haven't. That is, I'm not sure. It happened so quickly—George, I mean."

"He swept you off your feet!" she intoned dramatically.

"Don't make fun of me, Lina!" I exclaimed. "I'm so . . . And I *haven't* forgotten Carlo."

"But you must," she said seriously. "And no matter what you say, I believe you have, but you're too stubborn to admit it. My dear Leila"—she took my hands—"you don't need a Carlo in your life. Two artists in a single household—it would never, never do. I've told you that before, I know, but I cannot repeat it often enough."

"Mrs. Fowler said the same thing," I said. "I told her something about him, and she said one artist to a family was enough."

"She's a wise woman. I like her. Leila, look at it in its proper perspective. It was an infatuation, what you felt for Carlo, and it's ended as infatuations always do. It only needs for you to open your hands and let it go."

"Is that all?" I said slowly.

"Do you suppose that if you'd really loved him, you could have even looked at George?"

"I—I suppose not," I said.

"Of course not!" she agreed. "I'm very happy for you, Leila. You need someone like George. He's handsome, charming, steady, and wealthy. What more could you want?"

"Nothing, I suppose." I looked at Carlo's letter. His writing was small and neat. He was small, too. Besides the reality of George, he diminished even more. I said, "Nothing, Lina. I am really fortunate—and happy."

"You have every reason to be, my dear," she said.

That night Lina joined us for supper in the dining room and Mrs. Fowler toasted me in old champagne. I had felt very shy on seeing her, but she had embraced me warmly. "You're just what I wanted for my son," she had whispered. "I couldn't be more pleased. Spunk, that's what he needs!"

I had been extremely wary of Kezia's reaction, but she had kissed me on the forehead, saying, "I've heard I may call you Cousin, now." I must have looked dumbfounded, for she continued, "I've wanted to see George happy again and now I have."

After supper, at Mrs. Fowler's request, I sang for them in the music room and Lina was well enough to accompany me. It was a lovely evening, and meeting George's eyes as he turned the pages for Lina, I wondered at my earlier qualms and quibbles. I loved him, I was sure of that—loved him even more when after hearing about Carlo's offer, he said, "But we will all go to San Francisco then!"

The next week was full of practice and plans. George wanted the wedding to take place immediately, but I refused, for I had found that much as we think we know ourselves, I could not do what might have seemed the natural thing for me to do. I could not accept Mrs. Fowler's offer to be married at the Casa d'oro—I wanted her to meet my mother and my brother, and I wanted my wedding in my church at home. My decision pleased her.

"It's just as it ought to be," she had approved. "A girl needs her mother at a time like this."

George had been less sanguine. "I do not want to wait." He had frowned. "I want to call you *wife*." He had kissed me. "I want to possess you, now."

I wished he had not used that word—it reminded me of poor Millie's plaintive, "I wanted to be possessed by him." I had shivered, thinking of her fate and of Virginia Soames, as well.

"Why did you shiver?" he had demanded. "You're not afraid of me, are you?"

I had kissed him warmly. "Silly, no!"

"Then let's be married now," he had cried. "Oh, Leila"—he had seized my hands—"I couldn't lose you now."

"Darling, remember what I said about the lightning."

"Lightning?"

"Never in the same place twice."

It was finally decided that our wedding would take place in Denver on the first of May. An exchange of telegrams between Mama and the Fowlers, and arrangements were underway. Mama would make my wedding dress, but Mrs. Fowler insisted on buying me my trousseau in San Francisco—and since I was needed for rehearsals on the eighteenth of April, we planned to leave for the city on April eighth so that we might have time for sightseeing and for our preparations.

No one except Lina knew why I giggled when George mentioned we should be using his private railway car. Oddly enough, despite the luxury of my surroundings and my exquisite diamond engagement ring, that had been the first time I had actually realized I should be marrying the mogul of my dreams, and thinking about it, it still seemed as unreal as any dream. Events were happening too quickly for me. I wanted to put out my hands and stop them, but ten weak fingers could not halt an avalanche, and moments inexorably turned to hours, hours to days. By the time the last day came, I had almost become accustomed to hearing Mrs. Fowler blithely talk about sponsoring me in a series of concerts and at my Metropolitan debut. Later, she assured me, there would be appearances in Paris, Berlin, London, and Milan. She talked as glibly as Lina about coaches, language teachers, managers, music. Worth would make my dresses and my costumes, too. We would buy sables in Russia and I should go to the chateau country to buy the furniture for the New York townhouse she would give to George and myself. Her words were whirling in my head when finally I stood with Lina at a window in her room, looking at a full moon.

"Oh, Lina," I said wonderingly, "I shall have so much."

"Yes, indeed you will . . . . You should be very happy." A little anxiously, she said, "Are you happy, Leila?"

"More than I have any right to be," I answered.

"That's an odd way for you to put it."

"Is it?" I moved away from her. "Lina . . . I've a feeling . . . "

"What?"

"I—I'm frightened. It's all come so fast. I'd planned on at least a year of work and struggle . . . "

"At least a year," she echoed, smiling. "And it's happened in a month, instead. You can't complain about that."

"I'm not complaining. Still, it worries me."

"Why?"

"Shouldn't I have earned it, Lina? I haven't earned it yet. I haven't suffered, either. They say you must suffer for your art."

"There are many ways to suffer, Leila. You may not be as fortunate as you believe. Too much can sometimes be as bad as none at all. Too much can make you lazy and rob you of ambition. You might cease to work and cease to care."

"Oh, no!" I exclaimed. "I couldn't!"

"I hope not," she commented. "And indeed, I don't think you will. I have faith in you." She kissed me. "Now go to bed. We're rising early in the morning."

"You don't think I can sleep!" I exclaimed. "I shall watch the moon all night!"

"It's very bright," she said. "I advise you to pull your shades. You'll need your rest."

I did not take her advice. The moonlight was too beautiful to hide. In fact, I stood for a long time staring at the silvered trees; then, growing drowsy, I went to bed and dreamed of Carlo. It was an uncomfortable dream. We were back in the garden and I was telling him he must not kiss me because I was going to marry George. He looked at me furiously; his eyes grew large and more brilliant—of a sudden, they were Kezia's eyes. "You can't!" he said. His hands were at my throat. "You'll never sing again," he declared.

In my sleep, I screamed and tried to run away from him, but my feet were weighted as they are in dreams. I could not move, nor could I escape his hands as they fastened around my throat, pressing, while I cried out a second time, while I coughed and gagged and moaned, striving to be free of that terrible presence—which wasn't Carlo any longer! It was a fearful dream. I had to force myself awake. Finally my eyes were open, and between me and the moonlight was the shadow with the hands—the hands that were still clamped around my aching throat, the powerful thumbs pressed against my windpipe, shutting off air and sound and sight! I choked and gagged. My tongue seemed to be swelling in my mouth, and then dimly, dimly, I heard my name being called.

"Leila . . . Leila . . . " It was Lina—Lina's voice above the roaring in my ears.

I could not answer her, nor did the shadow move; the pressure increased. Lina must have run forward, for vaguely I was aware of a flurry of movement at the bed—but still the pressure continued. Suddenly it relaxed. I choked and coughed, but this time there was air to breathe. Lina knelt beside me. "Darling, darling, darling," she whispered. "Oh, Leila, I heard . . . I thought you were dreaming when you cried out. Still,

I came to see—thank God, I came to see . . . thank God . . . " She was weeping.

I could scarcely force a whisper through my agonized throat, but I had to know. "W-who . . . ? What . . . ?"

"I don't know. He—he wouldn't stop . . . . I couldn't get him to stop. I hit him with the poker. I might have killed him . . . . "

"Mus' fin' ligh—" I mumbled painfully. "Liiighht."

"Yes," she whispered, then added, "Hssssst . . . "; a draught had smote us from an opening door—the hall door. Lina quickly crouched down beside my bed, while I, with some difficulty, turned my head in time to see a tall figure in a long white gown enter quickly. In the moonlit darkness, I recognized Kezia Graves— Kezia Graves, the sleepwalker whom none dared disturb! Was she sleeping and walking, now? She moved soundlessly, but not aimlessly, in the direction of my bed. To this day I do not know what prompted me to hold my breath and lie so still. She glanced at me; her body shook as if she were laughing silently. She moved back, and in those monotonous cadences she had used that morning in her grandfather's room, she called, "John . . . John . . . I bid you come . . . John."

"What do you want here?" Lina cried loudly, leaping to her feet and brandishing the poker. "What are you doing in Leila's room?"

Kezia sprang back, then she began to scream— horrible piercing screams that echoed through the room. In her white gown and with her wild, wide eyes, she resembled a specter from some dark dimension of eternity.

She was still uttering her alarming shrieks when George and Mrs. Fowler came running down the hall. As they reached my room, I heard them cry. "She's walking in her sleep . . . . You mustn't be afraid, it's only Kezia in her sleep . . . . "But by that time Lina had found and pulled the light cord, and there was my bruised throat and there was the fallen form of John, the footman, who was beginning to show signs of returning consciousness and who, on waking, looked blankly about and asked us what he was doing in my room.

They took Kezia away and dragged John out, then Mrs. Fowler came back and gave me a drink. It was lukewarm and marvelously soothing to my aching throat. It had an odd taste, and I later learned it was her grandmother's concoction and that one of its principal properties was laudanum—it certainly made me sleep. I slept much of the following day and awakened to find Mrs. Parks ensconced by my bed—a much wider bed, I noted drowsily, than I had occupied in the sitting room of the Rose Suite. I also did not see the familiar tapestries or the rose silk draperies—this room was golden, and over its domed ceiling chased the chariot of the sun. Then I forgot my surroundings in the realization that my throat still ached abominably. I tried to talk but only succeeded in coming out with a croaking whisper. "My voice . . . my voice . . . " Tears filled my eyes.

Mrs. Parks bent over me, smiling. "No need to worry, honey," she soothed. Picking up a glass from a table by my bed and pressing it to my lips, she said, "Drink this. Doctor says it'll fix you up, right as a trivet."

Dutifully, I drank it. It felt wonderfully cool in my aching, throbbing throat. I slept again.

I awakened to find George sitting by my bed, looking pale and haggard. "Oh, my love," he said chokingly when he saw my eyes on him, "I—I almost lost you." Tears ran down his cheeks. "I should have died, too," he moaned.

I wished George were not so prone to weeping—it made me uncomfortable to see a man cry; but in this instance, I could understand. I whispered, "But you didn't. Here I am."

"Yes, my darling, my love." He took my hand and kissed the palm. "It was a miracle saved you!"

"It was Lina's ears."

"Lina, wonderful Lina!" he exclaimed. "If you only knew how much she's helped us!"

"How?"

"She . . . "

Unfortunately, Mrs. Parks chose that moment to return. "Now, now, George," she chided. "You know what the doctor said. Get along with you and let her rest."

"Not yet," I protested hoarsely. "I want to know . . ."

"All in good time," Mrs. Parks answered, "but no excitement. That's doctor's orders." She smiled at George and gave him a friendly little shove. "Scat."

With a lingering look at me, he went.

Mrs Parks sighed. "He's been beside himself, poor boy. It's a nine-day-wonder in town. Papers're full of it. Like father, like daughter, that's what I always said. Blood will tell."

"Tell me!" I urged.

She looked at me regretfully. "I'd sure like to," she said. "But not now . . . . Possess your soul in patience, honey. You'll know all there is to know, soon enough."

"Soon enough is not now!" I exclaimed, and then I was frightened again at the lingering hoarseness in my throat. I massaged it tenderly. "When . . . "

"You're going to be all right, baby," she assured me. " 'Nother day or two an' you'll sing like a bird."

"Will I?" I whispered.

"Take it from me," she said positively and pressed another glass of something on me.

Later, I awakened to find Lina and Mrs. Parks in my room. They were conversing in low voices, but I caught a word or two. " . . . away . . . " Lina said.

" . . . can't hold her . . . had to be crazy . . . "

"Who is crazy?" I demanded, and much to my surprise and pleasure, my voice sounded almost normal. "Oh!" I exclaimed. "I can speak again."

They both smiled at me. "Told'ya," Mrs. Parks said.

"Yes." Lina moved to me. "The doctor said the hoarseness ought to disappear by the third day."

"The third day?" I repeated. "Is it really the third day?" I looked toward the window but found instead a fireplace. "Where am I?"

"Mrs. Fowler thought you'd be more comfortable in here—the bed is wider. "It's called the Golden Suite," Lina explained.

"Oh. Kezia didn't show it to me that day . . . " I broke off. "Kezia . . ." I raised myself up and leaned back among what turned out to be a huge quantity of downy pillows. "I am much better!" I stated. "Now you'll have to tell me what happened. *Please?*"

They exchanged glances. "I expect we will," Mrs. Parks smiled. "Won't give neither of us no peace, less'n she knows." She looked at Lina rather regretfully. "Guess you oughta do the talkin' seein' as it was you figured out what happened."

Lina shook her head. "I yield the chair to you."

"Chair?" Mrs. Parks repeated blankly.

"She wants you to tell me!" I translated, "Please, *somebody* tell me!"

Mrs. Parks stared at Lina. "You're sure?"

"Mrs. Parks," I groaned. "Tell me!"

She gave a long contented sigh. "Well, it was the strangest thing. . . . I read *Trilby* when it come out, an' I said this wouldn't never happen in real life. I mean can you imagine that Svengali hypnotizin' that girl into an opera singer? Couldn't happen, that's what I says when I read that book. My husband, he said the same thing and so did Dr. Adams . . . "

" What has *Trilby* got to do with . . . ?" I began.

"Darling, shhh," Lina murmured.

"I just never thought it could happen, but it did. God knows where Kezia Graves learned . . . Well, actually, they're probably right, she learned to do it from her father. Must've watched him with his patients—he hypnotized people."

"Kezia hypnotized people?" I exclaimed.

"Yep." Mrs. Parks nodded. "Just like that there Svengali. It was Miss Lina guessed. Lookin' at poor John, she guessed, an' that doctor from the asylum come with Dr. Adams, he could do it, too, an' he did it to John . . . I watched. It was the curiousist thing . . . took out this little crystal pendant . . ." She reached for the watch she wore around her neck and swung it back and forth. "Like this," she said; "swung it like this, an' talked to John in this low creepy voice, an' John looked an' looked an' next thing you know, he'd dropped off like he was asleep—only when the doctor spoke to him, he could answer. . . ."

"Mrs. Parks!" I cried. "That's what Kezia did to me in her grandfather's room. She kept swinging her watch and talking in a low voice."

"Did she?" Lina cried. "You never told me."

"I never thought much about it afterward," I replied. "But that's what she must have tried to do. That's why she was so nice to me that afternoon. I knew there had to be a reason!"

"Thank God you're not a good subject!" Lina breathed.

"I wonder what she had in mind," Mrs. Parks said. "She was crazy . . . just plain crazy. An' when I think about poor Jacinto . . ."

"Jacinto . . ." I repeated. "He's the one who murdered Virginia Soames."

"It was Kezia murdered her," Mrs. Parks told me grimly. "That doctor from the asylum said she done it same's if she'd choked her herself. Murdered her like she tried to murder you. Should've heard poor John when he was under an' that doctor was talkin' to him. Kept sayin' 'Yes, Miss Kezia . . . yes, Miss Kezia . . .' an pretty soon he spilled the whole thing—how he was supposed to go to your room an' choke you an' when he woke up he wasn't supposed to know nothin' 'bout nothin' . . . . Didn't neither. Didn't know why George hit him so hard . . . didn't know anything. He's lucky. Weren't for Miss Lina, wouldn't nobody've believed him . . . might've been hanged just like poor Jacinto."

"How did you know?" I asked Lina.

"My brother . . ." she said. "He . . ."

"He's a magician and a hypnotist!" I exclaimed. "I remember."

"Yes," she said. "I used to watch him work with people. I could tell from John's actions what had happened, and also from the way that woman talked to him." She shivered.

"But why would she want to do such a thing?"

" 'Cause she's a dog in the manger, a mad dog!" Mrs. Parks said. "So crazy 'bout George she couldn't bear to see him with nobody else .... Should've heard her screamin' how she loved him ... said as how nobody should ever have him but her ... said as how he was hers 'cause she'd loved him all her life. . . . He was thunderstruck!" She shook her head. "You know, I been thinkin' about it ... Wouldn't be a bit surprised if she didn't have somethin' to do with the way poor little Millie Fairchild acted on her weddin' day. They was thick's thieves, her an' Kezia. . . ."

Lina's eyes were sad. "I would imagine she had everything to do with it, Mrs. Parks. She must have been more successful with her than she was with Leila —she put her under and gave her a mental suggestion."

I shuddered. "Otherwise she'd have murdered her, too."

"She did murder her, from what I hear," Lina said. "She killed her mind.'

"Killed her own as well,' Mrs. Parks snapped. "Ain't said two words since they locked her in that room—just sits there movin' them eyes about like she was her dead grandfather come to life. Always said she was the spittin' image of the old man. Mean as Hades, too. Goin' to the asylum this afternoon ... goin' to put her in a padded cell an' throw the key away. Talk about vipers in the bosom—poor George an' poor Mrs. Fowler . . ."

"Poor Kezia," Lina said. "I don't think she could help herself.

"Maybe not,' Mrs. Parks agreed. "What with seein' what happened to her ma an' all, right in front of her. Must've turned her queer. . . . She was crazy 'bout her father, too, from what I hear ... it was too danged much for her, I guess."

I looked at Lina. "Remember Mario," I said. "She must have been his *jettatura!*"

A Shadow on the House

I was able to get up that afternoon, and though I was a little weak, I was quite capable of walking—but George insisted on carrying me down to the garden. As luck would have it, we reached the front hall just as a doctor and an attendant were escorting Kezia outside. Her face was quite impassive—indeed, in her tailored suit and ugly hat, she looked much as I had first seen her at the station, except that her eyes no longer glittered; they had a fixed and glassy stare. Mrs. Fowler was with her, and I could see that she was trying to keep from crying. George, however, looked at his cousin without pity and hurried into the corridor.

As we went, Kezia said in a flat cold voice, "You'll never have him, either, Leila MacKenzie. I shall see to that."

The sound she uttered might have been intended for a laugh, but it chilled me to the bone. In my mind, I heard it all that day, and it threaded through my dreams at night. However, in the morning, it was gone. In the morning, I felt myself again, and more important, I could sing.

George and his mother were loathe to let me do it, but between us, Lina and I convinced them that I should never be happy unless I was allowed to sing Violetta in San Francisco—in the spring.

Part

FOUR

We left Sacramento at 7:30 on the morning of April seventeenth. We would arrive in San Francisco at one. Traveling with us were Agnes, Mrs. Fowler's maid; Bernard, who was George's valet; and Lucille, the maid who would be shared by Lina and me—mainly because Lina had refused her own attendant. I would have refused Lucille's services, too, but Lina had insisted I accept them. "It's a new life, Leila." she had told me, "and you must accustom yourself to it. You'll be very rich, you know."

"Um," I said unenthusiastically. I was in a strange mood, half-elated, half-frightened. In fact, I was thinking so much about our destination that I was hardly aware of my surroundings. Well, that is not entirely true. I must have noticed them because I described them in my journal—the luxurious appointments of that car, the wide, deep silken sofa, the thick carpets, the velvet curtains, the mahogany paneling, the huge plate-glass windows, the kitchen in the back. Yes, I wrote about that and about the scenery, too—the orange groves, the green fields, the gnarled trees, strange rocks, shining rivers, immense redwoods. But mainly I was looking inward to the past and forward to the future rather than outward at the present. I was thinking about the part I was to sing and about seeing the members of the troupe again. No, that is not true. I was thinking mainly if not entirely about Carlo Benedetto. Yes, seated very close to the man I would be marrying in less than a fortnight, I looked at the windows and seemed to see Carlo's face imprinted on the glass. Lina had written to him that I was to be married. She had received his congratulations, which she had passed along to me. He had also written that he was going to New York as soon as the San Francisco engagement ended. She had been delighted. "At last, he'll have his chance!" she had told me.

"Excited, dearest?" George pulled me a little closer to him.

"Very much." I smiled at him.

"Oh, Leila"—he kissed my ear—"I love you so very much."

"I love you," I told him. "With all my heart, I do!" But wrapped in his arms, I was not looking at him— I was staring at the window, willing Carlo's image to be gone, and as George kissed me, it finally disappeared.

We reached Oakland Pier on schedule. It was from there we would be ferried across the bay to San Francisco. As we walked aboard the ferry boat, the damp, salty, acrid smell of the sea was in my nostrils for the first time, and I looked incredulously at that vast, blue expanse that stretched endlessly across the horizon. I was at the threshold of the Golden Gate and it was so much more than all the pictures I had seen. During our brief crossing, I could hardly take my eyes from the sea—I scarcely glanced at the nearing city. Suddenly we were docking. There was a limousine awaiting us, and we were driven through narrow crowded streets to the Palace Hotel.

It was an immense place. We drove into a huge court, surrounded on three sides by tiers of balconies—I counted six—stretching up to a glassed-in roof. We were taken through a lobby which was all marble, glass, mirrors, potted palms, flowers, crystal chandeliers—I was dizzy before we reached our suite, but finally Lina and I were settled in our chamber. Lucille unobtrusively unpacked for us, and I suppose we talked but I cannot remember what we said. I was too excited by the proximity of Market Street below our windows—all crowded with clanging cable cars, chugging automobiles, carriages, and people. There were so many of them, going in all directions. All of a sudden I wanted to—I had to—join them!

"I must walk!" I told Lina.

"Oh," she sighed, "aren't you tired?"

"Tired?" I echoed. "When I've been sitting down all day? I shall fetch George and he shall take me walking." I practically danced out of our room into the parlor we shared with the Fowlers. George rose quickly from a chair.

"You look happy," he said, taking my hands. "Are you?"

I smiled up into his beautiful Byronic face. "Ecstatically!"

He kissed me. "You must always be happy, my darling," he murmured.

"I shall be particularly happy if you take me walking," I said.

"I will take you anywhere you choose," he said softly. "To the mountains of the Moon."

"I shall be happy with Chinatown," I replied. "It's not very far. I've looked at our guidebook. It's only a few blocks up Montgomery Street—at least it looks like a few blocks on the map."

He frowned. "Chinatown's known to be very dangerous."

"Not until after dark. Besides you're not afraid of danger, are you, George?"

"Danger? What danger?" Mrs. Fowler had emerged from her room.

"Chinatown, Mother. It's not safe," George said.

"Come, it's safe enough during the day. I'd like to go myself. Maybe I'll smoke a couple pipes of opium. Only we can't stay long, not if we're going to be back in time for the opera."

"The opera!" I exclaimed.

"Yep," she said, "saved it for a surprise. Caruso's singing in *Carmen*—hear he's a pretty good tenor."

"Oh, Mrs. Fowler!" I hugged her. "I've always wanted to hear him."

She kissed my cheek. "Thought as much, girlie. Just think—one of these days, you might be singing with him."

I was sure I had never been so happy as when we came back down into that beautiful lobby. We were on our way toward the door when I heard my name called in a voice I recognized. "Oh." I came to a dead stop. "Where is he?"

"Where is who?" George demanded.

I did not answer him. I was trying to locate him among the crowds that thronged the lobby, and suddenly he was at my elbow. "Carlo," I whispered, as he bowed over my hand.

"Good afternoon, Leila," he said. He looked as usual, well-groomed, well-dressed, but perhaps a little paler and thinner than I remembered—smaller, too, but perhaps that was because George was so tall. The contrast between the two men was marked. George would be noticed anywhere—Carlo could easily be lost in any crowd.

Moving a little closer to George, I said, "Good afternoon, Carlo. You remember Mrs. and Mr. Fowler, don't you?"

At the end of an exchange of polite greetings, Carlo said, "I wondered if I would see you. I was not sure—it is such a mammoth place."

"Isn't it lovely?" I exclaimed. "We have the corner suite—501—in case you want to speak to Lina. She's up there now."

"Alas, I shall have to wait until tomorrow morning. I am here to see an old friend from Italy, who has also a suite in this establishment."

"That wouldn't be Caruso, would it?" Mrs. Fowler asked. "I heard one of the bellboys talking about how he was here."

Carlo smiled. "As it happens, Madame, it would be Caruso."

"You know him?" I asked.

"For many years," Carlo replied. "I knew him in Italy before he was famous."

"I guess you Italians all know each other," George said.

There was nothing ostensibly wrong with his remark, yet I did not like it—to me it was vaguely offensive. I said quickly, "They do if they're in music, George—the opera world is very small." I looked at Carlo and found him staring at me, a flicker of surprise in his eyes. He looked away quickly.

"Yes," he agreed, "that is true. It is a very small world." He bowed to the Fowlers. "I must go. I am so pleased to have met you all again. Oh, and I must offer you, sir, my congratulations—and you, too, Leila—on your approaching nuptials. I was delighted when Lina wrote to me about it. I wish you very happy."

"Thank you," I said. "I will be seeing you at rehearsal tomorrow."

He nodded. "I shall assuredly be there." He smiled.

"Do give my best wishes to the Maestro," I told him.

"I shall, of course." He bowed and was gone among the crowds. I did not watch to see if he looked back.

George said, "He was the man who would not let you remain in the company."

"Yes," I said.

His eyes glinted. "I should have expressed my thanks." He took my arm. "I owe a great deal to him."

I knew what he wanted me to say and I said it. "So do I."

"And so do I," Mrs. Fowler echoed, smiling at me. Then we went out into the teeming, confusing, exciting streets of San Francisco and I almost succeeded in forgetting Carlo.

The opera was very nearly everything I had expected. The house was huge, and from our box, which was directly over the stage, we looked around at a glitter of diamonds. In common with Mrs. Fowler, who was aglow with her own collection, women wore them on ears, throat, chest, shoulders, arms, waist, in a blue-white blaze that was, coupled with the lights, dazzling and distracting. There were flowers throughout the house; baskets of roses rimmed the pit, and there were orchids and other blossoms blooming near the boxes. Everyone was magnificently dressed. I was glad I was sitting in a box, for some of the ladies wore plumes in their high pompadours, and sitting behind them, it would have been impossible to see the stage.

I did notice, as I looked about me, that eyes were straying toward our box—eyes, often augmented by opera glasses or lorgnettes, held in the hands of some of those elegant women. I knew, too, that I was not the object of their admiration or curiosity—it was George, who looked spectacular in his evening clothes, his resemblance to Byron even more pronounced. To do him justice, he was entirely unaware of their scrutiny. His eyes were on me and he whispered, "You are the most beautiful woman here, my darling. The most beautiful woman in the world. One day, I shall dress you from head to toe in diamonds."

I laughed. "My goodness, I'd be weighted down. This ring is enough." I held it out, and its huge pear-shaped stone, catching the light, made me blink.

George kissed my hand. "I love you."

"I love you, too." I answered. To myself, I added, "I do. I really do." I smiled at him. In that moment, the houselights dimmed, the conductor took his place, raised his baton, and the overture to *Carmen* filled the house. Alfred Hertz was on the podium that night—to my mind, Carlo would have been the better choice.

I could find no fault with the stage decor. The backdrops were brilliantly painted and an entire square in Seville was marvelously reproduced—even to caballeros riding by on horseback. The stage was crowded with groups of people in Spanish costumes, soldiers in their bright uniforms—it was wonderful. I was not impressed with my first sight of Enrico Caruso; he was small, dumpy and even bunchy in his uniform, but his eyes were attractive—large and bright. At his first few phrases, I forgot all about his appearance; his voice was as thrilling as it had been reported to be. I leaned forward—there was a similar movement over the entire house, as opera glasses were trained on the stage and collective sighs of appreciation were heard. I am afraid, however, that I nearly burst out laughing when the Carmen made her first appearance. As George muttered, she was clearly a gypsy who liked her meat and potatoes, for the woman, Olive Fremstad, was immense. She lumbered rather than walked across the stage, her red satin costume stretched over a huge bosom and a swelling stomach. She had a rich mezzo, but she did not sing with any enthusiasm or interpretation and her French was abominable! Furthermore, since I was so very close to the stage I could see that the glances she directed at her lover were anything but passionate; she seemed to dislike him heartily, while he was supremely indifferent to her—and, indeed, who could blame him?

Still, by the fourth act, when Carmen lay dead with Don José keening over her fallen bulk, I managed to squeeze out a tear—not so much for her as for the glorious voice of the tenor, who had deserved every bravo and every flower that had pelted the stage. We waited through the curtain calls. I clapped until my hands ached, and even after the curtain came down for the last time and the people started leaving, I stayed. It was my first time inside a major opera house, and if my happiness was incomplete, it was only because I was not beside Caruso, taking bows in place of Madame Fremstad. But I soon should be—had not Mrs. Fowler promised to arrange it? Soon I should have everything I had ever wanted! Everything! I glanced down at the deserted podium. Everything, I said defiantly.

Since I had to rehearse the following morning, we did not stay out late. Besides, Lina was tired. We had a light supper of oysters, squabs, salad, sherbert, cakes, and champagne, and we returned to the hotel about one-thirty in the morning. I remember that just before I went to bed, Lina said, "You looked radiant tonight, child. You and George reminded me of the prince and princess in some fairy tale—and I know you'll live happily every after."

"I am sure we shall," I said, Yet, when I lay in bed, I thought of those words "happily ever after." I asked myself, will we? Myself replied staunchly, "Of course!" On that note, I went to sleep and dreamed of Carlo in Spanish costume being borne off by the immense Madame Fremstad, who was riding a huge stallion —then, suddenly, her steed galloped back and, leaping over my head, landed squarely on my pillow! I felt the thump of its hooves—they grazed my cheek. The impact awakened me, and I sat up to find the bed shaking, while around me there was a great roaring sound. Something crashed. It was a table across the room. Incredibly the floor was heaving up and down as if the whole hotel had suddenly become a storm-tossed ship. Another crash alerted me to the other side of the room, where the armoire had turned over on its side. Dazedly, I realized that my nighttable was lying on my pillow.

"Leila." Lina screamed. "Leila, are you all right?"

I looked wildly into the dimness and failed to find her bed. "Yes," I yelled back. "But where are you? And what is happening?"

"Earthquake!" she cried.

A few seconds—or perhaps it was minutes, I don't know—and the quivering had stopped, but the air was full of a babble of voices inside the hotel and outside on the street below.

Lina stumbled over to my bed. We grabbed each other. "Thank God, you're not hurt!" we cried simultaneously. Then we rushed to the window and stared down. Hundreds of people were running from the hotel, some still in their night clothes, others in oddly assorted garments, and a few in barely anything! Across the street, a building had crumbled and I heard terrible wailing shrieks and groans. The air was full of screaming. Shuddering, I turned away. Lina followed me.

"Dressed . . . we have to get dressed," she said.

It was impossible to extract our clothes from the armoire—it had fallen on its face and was too heavy to budge—but I did see a drawer lying in the middle of the room. In it, I found a shirtwaist and skirt. It was not until hours later that I realized I had put them on over my nightgown. Lina was forced to don the gown she had worn the night before, but she had discovered two shawls, one of which she was handing to me when she suddenly froze, muttering, "God, what is *that?*"

I had just heard it, too—a frightful wailing scream that chilled me to the bone. It was coming from our parlor! "Mrs. Fowler!" I gasped, rushing for the door. It was not there. I stepped onto it, nearly falling, and righted myself by grabbing at something that turned out to be an upturned desk. I picked my way around more broken furniture and shattered glass toward that sound, which was coming, I now realized, from George's room! Had he been killed? Finally, I reached the door. It was half off its hinges, and Mrs. Fowler was standing inside. My heart sank. It was she who was making that terrible noise—and her son must be dead, but she was not crying! She was standing, motionless, staring straight ahead of her, at the bed—at the man crouched against the headboard, clutching his pillow and screaming like a terrified child.

"Has . . . has he been hurt?" I demanded.

Mrs. Fowler shook her head. "Nope," she said; "he —he's scared." Her voice trembled. "Scared to death— went all to pieces when the quake hit. I can't do a thing with him." Her voice broke, and she burst into tears. I put an arm around her. I did not want to look at George, but I had to. I tried to speak gently; I tried to keep the contempt from my voice, but I fear I was only partially successful. I said, "You'd better get dressed, George. We have to get out of here. Everybody's getting out."

If he heard me, he gave no sign of it. His terrified wails continued, and his mother, going to the bed, put her arms around him protectively. "Georgie . . . Georgie, lamb." She patted his shoulder and he clutched her, burrowing his head in her bosom.

"Mama . . . Mama . . . Mama . . ." he sobbed.

"It's all right, honey. . . . It's all over and we have to get dressed now. . . . There's no telling what's going to happen, no telling at all. Baby, baby, stop crying, we have to get out of here, that's a good boy."

I watched transfixed, but Lina, who had been standing just behind me on that shattered threshold, began to cry. I whirled around.

"Don't!" I commanded fiercely. "Please don't, Lina!" I came out of the bedroom. "I—we . . . we have to do something. . . ." I looked at her, trying to collect my scattered thoughts.

"Leila! Leila!" someone called. It was a man. George? It could not be George—I could still hear him whimpering. "Leila! Leila, where are you?"

"In here . . . she's in here." It was Lina who had answered.

"Oh, God, what's happened to her?" A slight, disheveled figure rushed into the room. He was clad in a blood-stained white shirt and dusty black trousers; his hair was wild and a long red scratch ran down the side of his face.

"Carlo!" I shrieked. "Carlo, Carlo, Carlo!" Running to him, I threw my arms around him.

He looked at me incredulously. "Oh, God, you are safe . . . *cara mia, carissima* . . . safe . . ."

"Yes, my darling, my darling, I'm safe. But you—you're bleeding . . . you've been hurt . . . your cheek . . ." I touched it and my hand was stained with blood.

"It is nothing," he said. "A scratch, nothing . . . nothing." He kissed me not once but many times, *"Cara, cara, cara,"* he murmured; then suddenly he stopped. "I have no right—you are . . ."

"I am nothing!" I told him, moving closer to him. "I love you. I always, always have. I don't care if it isn't right. I don't care if I'm an artist and you're another. I love you!"

His arms were around me, holding me so tightly, I could hardly breathe. "When this happened, I thought first of you. I have loved you a long time, but . . . Oh, none of this matters, my Leila . . . . You are mine and you are alive. I feared to find you dead, my love." He released me then. "But we must get out of here—

through this city, already there is fire." He looked around. "Where is Lina?"

"I am here," she said. "I'm ready." She looked at me. "I believe George is calmer. His mother is dressing him."

Carlo gave her a startled glance. "His mother . . ."

"It doesn't matter," I said hastily. I did not want to talk or even think about George. He had ceased to have any reality for me. The only reality was Carlo, and I knew that if he had not come to me, I should have gone to him. I kissed him again. "Darling," I said tearfully, "I am so glad . . . so glad . . ." I began to cry.

"*Cara,* don't." His lips were against my hair, then he stiffened, looking over my shoulder.

I turned to find Mrs. Fowler watching us. Her eyes were tragic. She said, "You'd better hightail it out of here, girlie. I can manage George, so don't worry your head about him. Always said you had a lot of spunk. Wished he did, too. Never did, though. Never had any at all." Her voice trembled.

I could not say anything. I could only go to her and embrace her gently. I did not look toward the bedroom. I went back to Carlo and Lina, and together we made our way down the broken staircase of the Palace Hotel and into those crowded but strangely quiet streets. People had ceased to scream. Shocked into silence, carrying all manner of belongings—jewelry, paintings, lamps, clothing—they walked singly or in little knots, avoiding debris and fallen bodies. On either side of us there was terrible devastation—roofs had caved in, foundations had crumbled, street lights lay twisted and shattered, train tracks were uprooted and bent into grotesque shapes; there were great fissures in the pavement, and the air was filled with noxious odors, mainly escaping gas and burning wood. A cloud of smoke was beginning to enshroud the city, but I was not afraid—safety, in the form of Carlo Benedetto, strode at my side.

It was not until hours later, when through Carlo's

conniving we had been rowed back across the bay to Oakland and were on board an outbound train, that we learned about his fruitless attempt to rescue the Maestro from beneath the wall that had collapsed on his bed. As for the company, most of it, he believed, was safe. He wept then for the Maestro—silently and a little abashedly because tears, he said, were for women only. I could have told him differently, but I did not— I owed that much to the man who had loved me. I was even grateful for his weeping, for it had set me free.

Lina was wrong! It is an ideal marriage—a prima donna and a celebrated conductor; Carlo's reviews have been ecstatic! Recently, Lina came to visit us in New York. We live at the Ansonia Hotel in a lovely apartment! "Come on, admit it," I said to her. "Aren't Carlo and I divinely happy?"

She looked at me and laughed. "But darling"—she began—"you're not . . ."

"Oh," I interrupted, "I know what you're going to say, but I have every intention—when my precious little Paulina is older. . . . My voice has deepened and matured—you've said so yourself! After all, I'm just twenty . . ." Then I blushed, and I dared not tell her why. But when our boy is born—I am sure he will be a boy—I shall be only twenty-one . . . twenty-two or -three before I would trust my angel to a nurse, but that's young enough to have a very long career. Meanwhile, I am practicing Tosca, Leonora, and Amelia with Carlo, and he agrees I shall be famous yet!

Other SIGNET Gothics You'll Want to Read

☐ **THE SPECTRAL BRIDE (formerly titled The Fetch) by Margaret Campbell.** Were they following the longings of their hearts or the spell of a family curse—an ancient cry for vengeance that must be fulfilled . . . ?
(#Y6431—$1.25)

☐ **THE BROKEN KEY by Mary Linn Roby.** Could Sara hope to find love in this gloomy mansion where terror reigned . . . ? (#Q5916—95¢)

☐ **THE HOUSE AT KILGALLEN by Mary Linn Roby.** Lovely Mara Hanley had no stake in the Kilgallen inheritance. But all too soon the greed that poisoned the lowering mansion reached out to trap her in a web of evil. She longed to flee the menacing house—but love held her captive! (#T5671—75¢)

☐ **WOMAN IN BLACK by Monica Heath.** Julie had come West expecting a loving reunion with her father. Instead she was faced with tragedy and terror and found herself falling in love with a strange but irresistible man who might lead her to her doom. . . . (#Q6073—95¢)

☐ **STONEHAVEN by Elizabeth St. Clair.** Bewitched by a handsome young stranger, Tamara Lewis found herself the bride of a man she hardly knew and the mistress of a gloomy old mansion dominated by an ancient curse. (#Q5946—95¢)

THE NEW AMERICAN LIBRARY, INC.,
P.O. Box 999, Bergenfield, New Jersey 07621

Please send me the SIGNET BOOKS I have checked above. I am enclosing $_____ (check or money order—no currency or C.O.D.'s). Please include the list price plus 25¢ a copy to cover handling and mailing costs. (Prices and numbers are subject to change without notice.)

Name_____

Address_____

City_____ State_____ Zip Code_____
Allow at least 3 weeks for delivery

Have You Read These Bestsellers from Signet?

☐ **FEAR OF FLYING by Erica Jong.** A dazzling uninhibited novel that exposes a woman's most intimate sexual feelings. . . . "A sexual frankness that belongs to and hilariously extends the tradition of **Catcher in the Rye** and **Portnoy's Complaint** . . . it has class and sass, brightness and bite."—John Updike, New Yorker (#J6139—$1.95)

☐ **PENTIMENTO by Lillian Hellman.** Hollywood in the days of Sam Goldwyn . . . New York in the glittering times of Dorothy Parker and Tallulah Bankhead . . . a 30-year love affair with Dashiel Hammett, and a distinguished career as a playwright. "Exquisite . . . brilliantly finished . . . it will be a long time before we have another book of personal reminiscence as engaging as this one."—**New York Times Book Review** (#J6091—$1.95)

☐ **CARRIE by Stephen King.** The psychic terror of Rosemary's Baby! The sexual violence of The Exorcist! A novel of a girl possessed of a terrifying power . . . "Gory and horrifying . . . you can't put it down!"—Chicago Tribune
(#E6410—$1.75)

☐ **HARRIET SAID by Beryl Bainbridge.** An explosive shocker about little girls. . . . Here is the horror of child's play mixed with erotic manipulation and evil possession. "A highly plotted horror tale that ranks with the celebrated thrillers of corrupt childhood."—New York Times Book Review
(#W6058—$1.50)

☐ **THE FRENCH LIEUTENANT'S WOMAN by John Fowles.** By the author of **The Collector** and **The Magus**, a haunting love story of the Victorian era. Over one year on the N.Y. Times Bestseller List and an international bestseller. "Filled with enchanting mysteries, charged with erotic possibilities . . ." —Christopher Lehmann-Haupt, N.Y. Times
(#E6484—$1.75)

THE NEW AMERICAN LIBRARY, INC.,
P.O. Box 999, Bergenfield, New Jersey 07621

Please send me the SIGNET BOOKS I have checked above. I am enclosing
$_____(check or money order—no currency or C.O.D.'s). Please include the list price plus 25¢ a copy to cover handling and mailing costs. (Prices and numbers are subject to change without notice.)

Name_____

Address_____

City_____ State_____ Zip Code_____

Allow at least 3 weeks for delivery

More Bestsellers from SIGNET

☐ **ELIZABETH AND CATHERINE by Robert Coughlan.** For the millions enthralled by **Nicholas & Alexandra**, the glittering lives and loves of the two Russian Empresses who scandalized the world and made a nation . . . "Fascinating!"—**The Boston Globe.** A Putnam Award Book and a Literary Guild Featured Alternate.
(#J6455—$1.95)

☐ **CONUNDRUM by Jan Morris.** The incredible and moving story of a man who was transformed into a woman. . . . "Certainly the best first-hand account ever written by a traveler across the boundaries of sex."—**Newsweek** (#W6413—$1.50)

☐ **LAST RIGHTS by Marya Mannes.** A brilliant writer makes an eloquent plea for the dying and their right to a dignified death. . . . "A book to read and to pass on to others . . . passionate and direct."—**The New York Times** (#W6306—$1.50)

☐ **A CIRCLE OF CHILDREN by Mary MacCracken.** A moving story of how a teacher's dedication and love worked miracles with her emotionally disturbed children. "We finish the book shaken yet uplifted, for we have watched how love and understanding, working together, can produce what were once called miracles."—Clifton Fadiman, in **Book-of-the-Month-Club News**
(#W6354—$1.50)

☐ **THE SWARM by Arthur Herzog.** A masterpiece of chilling terror. "For those who relished **The Andromeda Strain**, a suspense story of death and destruction wrought by a new, deadly species of bee."—**Washington Post Book World** (#J6351—$1.95)

THE NEW AMERICAN LIBRARY, INC.,
P.O. Box 999, Bergenfield, New Jersey 07621

Please send me the SIGNET BOOKS I have checked above. I am enclosing $_____(check or money order—no currency or C.O.D.'s). Please include the list price plus 25¢ a copy to cover handling and mailing costs. (Prices and numbers are subject to change without notice.)

Name_____

Address_____

City_____State_____Zip Code_____
Allow at least 3 weeks for delivery

EVOKE THE WISDOM OF THE TAROT

With your own set of 78, full-color cards—the Rider-Waite deck you have studied in THE TAROT REVEALED.

ORDER FORM

The New American Library, Inc.
P.O. Box 999
Bergenfield, New Jersey 07621

Gentlemen:
Please send me_____Tarot deck(s) priced at $6.00 each, plus $1.05 per deck for postage and handling.

I am enclosing my (check) (money order) for $_____
to cover the cost of the above order.

NAME_____

ADDRESS_____

CITY_____STATE_____ZIP_____
(please type or print)

Offer valid only in the United States of America